DESERT FURY

Rodelo went into a low dive, his powerful right shoulder catching Harbin on the hip and knocking him spinning to the ground. Before he could get a good grip on his gun again, Rodelo kicked it from his hand.

With a grunted oath, Harbin came off the sand in a lunge, but he pulled his punch too wide and Dan Rodelo caught him on the cheekbone with a wicked right as he came in. Harbin, stopped in his tracks, was perfectly set up for the sweeping left, and he went down hard.

Stunned, he lay still for a moment. When he got up he was quiet. "All right, Rodelo," he said. "I'll kill you for that."

Bantam Books by Louis L'Amour

NOVELS

Bendigo Shafter
Borden Chantry
Brionne
The Broken Gun
The Burning Hills
The Californios
Callaghen
Catlow
Chancy
The Cherokee Trail
Comstock Lode
Conagher
Crossfire Trail
Dark Canyon
Down the Long Hills
The Empty Land
Fair Blows the Wind
Fallon
The Ferguson Rifle
The First Fast Draw
Flint
Guns of the Timberlands
Hanging Woman Creek
The Haunted Mesa
Heller with a Gun
The High Graders
High Lonesome
Hondo
How the West Was Won
The Iron Marshal
The Key-Lock Man
Kid Rodelo
Kilkenny
Killoe
Kilrone
Kiowa Trail
Last of the Breed
Last Stand at Papago Wells
The Lonesome Gods
The Man Called Noon
The Man from Skibbereen
The Man from the Broken Hills
Matagorda
Milo Talon
The Mountain Valley War
North to the Rails
Over on the Dry Side
Passin' Through
The Proving Trail
The Quick and the Dead
Radigan
Reilly's Luck
The Rider of Lost Creek
Rivers West
The Shadow Riders
Shalako
Showdown at Yellow Butte
Silver Canyon
Sitka
Son of a Wanted Man
Taggart
The Tall Stranger
To Tame a Land
Tucker
Under the Sweetwater Rim
Utah Blaine
The Walking Drum
Westward the Tide
Where the Long Grass Blows
War Party
West from Singapore
West of Dodge
With These Hands
Yondering

SHORT STORY COLLECTIONS

Beyond the Great Snow Mountains
Bowdrie
Bowdrie's Law
Buckskin Run
The Collected Short Stories of Louis L'Amour (vols. 1–7)
Dutchman's Flat
End of the Drive
From the Listening Hills
The Hills of Homicide
Law of the Desert Born
Long Ride Home
Lonigan
May There Be a Road
Monument Rock
Night Over the Solomons
Off the Mangrove Coast
The Outlaws of Mesquite
The Rider of the Ruby Hills
Riding for the Brand
The Strong Shall Live
The Trail to Crazy Man
Valley of the Sun

SACKETT TITLES

Sackett's Land
To the Far Blue Mountains
The Warrior's Path
Jubal Sackett
Ride the River
The Daybreakers
Sackett
Lando
Mojave Crossing
Mustang Man
The Lonely Men
Galloway
Treasure Mountain
Lonely on the Mountain
Ride the Dark Trail
The Sackett Brand
The Sky-Liners

THE HOPALONG CASSIDY NOVELS

The Riders of High Rock
The Rustlers of West Fork
The Trail to Seven Pines
Trouble Shooter

NONFICTION

Education of a Wandering Man
Frontier
The Sackett Companion: A Personal Guide to the Sackett Novels
A Trail of Memories: The Quotations of Louis L'Amour, compiled by Angelique L'Amour

POETRY

Smoke from This Altar

LOST TREASURES

Louis L'Amour's Lost Treasures: Volume 1

KID RODELO

A NOVEL

Louis L'Amour

Postscript by Beau L'Amour

BANTAM BOOKS
NEW YORK

2018 Bantam Books Mass Market Edition

Published in the United States by Bantam Books, an imprint of Random House, a division of Penguin Random House LLC, New York.

BANTAM and the HOUSE colophon are registered trademarks of Penguin Random House LLC.

Originally published in the United States by Bantam Books, an imprint of Random House, a division of Penguin Random House LLC, in 1966.

ISBN 978-0-525-48628-2
ebook ISBN 978-0-525-48636-7

Cover art: Gordon Crabb

Printed in the United States of America

randomhousebooks.com

9 8 7 6 5 4 3 2 1

Bantam Books mass market edition: July 2018

Kid Rodelo

CALIFORNIA
MEXICO
Yuma
Territorial Prison
Colorado River
YUMA
Gila River
GILA MOUNTAINS
Gold City
YUMA DESERT
Cipriano Pass
Raven's Butte Tank
Raven's Butte
Lechuguilla Desert
ARIZONA
MEXICO
Tinajas Altas
Camino de Diablo
TINAJA ALTAS MOUNTAINS
EL GRAN DESIERTO
Rio Colorado
S O
Puerto Isabel
BAJA CALIFORNIA
WESTERN SONORA
Scale of Miles
0 5 10 15 20
GULF

Map by Alan McKnight

Kid Rodelo

CHAPTER 1

THE YUMA DESERT, east of the Colorado River mouth, was like the floor of a furnace; but of the four riders, three were Yaqui Indians and accustomed to the heat, as were the buzzards swinging in lazy circles above them. The fourth rider did not mind the heat. He was dead.

The part of the desert they were now crossing was hard sand. Before them and on their right were sand dunes. Four days earlier the dead man had ridden his horse to death in those dunes. Obsessed by the desire to escape, to reach the boat awaiting him on Adair Bay, he had not realized until too late how hard he had ridden the animal.

To attempt the escape across the desert, dotted here and there by low-growing creosote or burro bush, was madness if he traveled by day. Yet there was no time to stop. It was the Yaquis, hungry for the fifty dollars his carcass would bring, who arranged his schedule. It was run or die, and so he ran . . . and died anyway, for they caught up with him short of his goal.

Nobody escaped across the Yuma Desert. The Yaqui in the battered cavalry hat could have told him that, for he had collected bounty on seventeen bodies, and it made a nice living. The Yaquis knew nothing about the boat on Adair Bay, and cared less.

At Yuma Prison, Tom Badger did know about the boat. He had been the escaped prisoner's only confidant, had known of the plans, and had known that the boat was to appear at a certain place on the shore each evening for two weeks. The men handling the boat were well paid, and they knew only that one man, perhaps two or more, would appear out of the desert. They were to pick those men up, ask no questions, and sail them to Mazatlan.

Tom Badger had intended to make the break with Isacher, but Isacher was alone when the chance came and he accepted the chance. Badger had been left behind, but he did not blame his cell mate. In his place he would have done the same thing. Now he waited. . . . Had Isacher made it?

Suddenly he heard the bell toll. One . . . two . . . three . . . four!

The prison gate had opened and closed. Badger sat up, scratching. Somebody had come in, and at this hour? It was not quite six in the morning.

Outside he heard a voice, some distance off and near the gate. It was plain enough, even at the distance, for in this clear air sounds carry. "They brought in another one."

"Who is it?"

"Who d'you think? Only one man's escaped from here in six months."

Isacher!

Tom Badger held himself very still, his mind suddenly clear. Isacher was dead, and there were days to go before the boat would leave Adair Bay. Isacher had been clear about that, and had planned to arrive on the first of the fourteen days the boat would spend in the bay. Those other thirteen days were simply insurance against any delay or mistake in timing.

Whoever was in that boat could know nothing of Isacher's failure. Therefore if one or more men should arrive at Adair Bay, the boat would pick them up and take them to Mazatlan. Isacher had failed, but his death left the door open.

Badger's thoughts were interrupted by a jangle of keys and tramping feet. Doors opened and he heard the guards turning the convicts out for the day's work.

Miller came in with the day man and began unlocking the leg-irons that chained them to the floor.

Gopher looked up, whining, "I just can't make it today. I—"

"Shut up!" Tom Badger looked down irritably. Joe Harbin was all right, but Gopher could do nothing but whine.

"Get your boots on!" The jailer was impatient. He was a hard man who allowed no leeway for any of them. Miller, on the other hand, was a good guard and a fair one. If a con did not make it hard for Miller, he was inclined to give him any breaks the rules would allow.

"I can't—"

The jailer nudged Gopher with a boot. "On your feet!"

"Please!"

The jailer raised the keys to strike, but Miller interposed. "Lay off him. He took ten lashes yesterday."

"And now he's askin' for ten more."

"Get your boots on, son," Miller said. "Go let the Doc have a look at you."

Slowly, painfully, Gopher pulled on his boots and got to his feet, lining up in the prison corridor with the others.

As they marched down the corridor he stared into the cells of the less troublesome prisoners. In each of them he saw men who were freshly shaved making up comfortable bunks. At least, they were comfortable compared to the hard stone floor on which he had slept in the maximum security cell. Halted briefly, the three saw Danny Rodelo. He was stripped to the waist while the doctor checked him over.

Miller watched for a moment. "Doc?"

"Just a minute, guard. I have to check this man for release. He's going out today."

"Lucky stiff," somebody muttered, and Miller glanced around at the faces of the convicts, but there was no indication who had made the comment, and he did not press the question.

Rodelo was lucky to get out, any man was. In the case of Dan Rodelo, however, it had just been bad luck that ever got him in. He was, as all the prisoners knew, no criminal at all.

Rough, yes . . . and tough. He was a man who would make it the hard way if necessary, and anybody who bought a piece of his action bought trouble. Rodelo had done his time standing up. Never a complaint, never an argument. He did his work every day, and every day's work was a good one.

"All right, Rodelo."

Dr. Wilson took up his bag and stepped into the corridor. "What is it, Miller?"

"This man—he claims he's sick."

Dr. Wilson glanced at Gopher. "Oh, it's you, is it?" Lifting the man's shirt he looked at the scrawny back, laced with the marks of the lashes. "Healing all right."

Dan Rodelo pulled on his shirt while the others watched. He tucked it under his belt and reached for a necktie.

Joe Harbin stared at him angrily, then started to speak, but Tom Badger nudged him sharply and Joe closed his mouth.

"You're fit enough," Wilson said to Gopher. "You'd better keep working or that back will stiffen up."

"You mean I've got to work?"

"Everybody works in here, son. Stay out of trouble and one of these days you'll walk out of here just like Rodelo is. If you make trouble you'll just get one lashing after another, and when you get out you'll be ready for the bone yard. Take it from me—I see them all."

Dan Rodelo stood watching them go, then stepped out into the corridor and walked along to the warden's office. He was aware of the stares of envy from those he left behind, but he knew few of them, and had little in common with any of them.

He stopped suddenly. Three Yaquis were bringing in a body. Despite himself, he stared at the dead face. He knew the man . . . knew him simply because there was only one man it could be. There was little about the cadaver he looked upon that resembled the man he had known by sight.

There had been rumors about Isacher. He had relatives back East who had money, and there was a story that some cash had been spread around. It was still a mystery as to how he had crashed out.

The prison clerk opened the door to the warden's office. "Isacher's body, sir, for your identification."

"Can't you identify him?"

"Regulations, sir. It is required that you see the body."

The warden came to the door and looked down at the dead man. A slender, attractive man in his late fifties, his military bearing indicating his background, the warden had no liking for the task. "I'd never recognize him," he commented. "He must have gone through hell."

"Have you seen that desert to the south? I don't think there's anything like it anywhere else in North America. He was probably half dead from thirst when they shot him."

The warden turned away. "They always do shoot them, don't they?"

"A dead man can't drink their water, sir, and down there water is almighty scarce."

"All right, get him out of here. See that he's properly buried." As an afterthought, he added, "And be sure you can locate the grave. His family may want the body, although I doubt it."

The Yaqui in the cavalry hat stepped forward. "*Oro?*"

"Pay him," the warden said. "Here . . . I'll sign that."

He signed the voucher, then glanced up at the clerk. "I will sign," he said, "but I will be damned if I approve. No matter what they were guilty of, it simply isn't right to have them hunted down and killed."

The clerk was cynical. "That's how these Yaquis live, sir. I mean the outfit that hang around the fort." He paused. "I've often thought we should recruit them, sir, train them into good soldiers. They have the makings."

"Bloodthirsty savages."

"Some of them."

The Indian took his money and turned away, and as he did so he saw Dan Rodelo. For an instant their eyes held, the Yaqui recognizing the dislike showing in Rodelo's eyes, and letting his own gaze travel down over Rodelo's outfit. For a convict, which the Yaqui knew he was, he was dressed very well. The new boots were polished and shining.

The Indian pointed at them. "I have." He looked up at Rodelo. "You see. Someday I have."

"Sorry," Rodelo replied, "I'm going out the gate. I am free."

Rodelo walked past the Yaqui and stopped in front of the warden's desk. Something in Rodelo recognized the warden for what he was, and almost instinctively he stood at attention.

"Well, Rodelo?" The warden studied him for a moment. "You were in the Army?"

"Yes, sir. The Fifth Cavalry, sir."

The clerk came to the desk with a brown paper sack and placed it before Rodelo. Dan glanced down . . . the sack contained his possessions, and they were very few. He put them in his pockets without comment, then belted on the holster and gun belt that came with the sack.

The warden took a five-dollar gold piece from a drawer and handed it to Rodelo. "Here's your discharge money. I am glad to see you leaving here, Rodelo, and I hope you do nothing to bring you back."

"I've had enough, sir." He hesitated. "It was nothing criminal, when it comes to that."

"I know. I checked your record."

The warden seemed reluctant to let him go. "Rodelo, these are trying times. Any time of transition is sure to develop situations that are difficult to handle, but remember that our country is changing. We cannot live by the gun any longer.

"We have settlers coming from the East every day, we have businessmen wanting to invest. We must learn to settle our disputes without gunplay, and we must leave the apprehension of criminals to the law."

"I know, sir."

"I hope you do, Rodelo, for I think you're a good man. Stay out of trouble." He looked directly into Rodelo's eyes. "And stay away from bad company."

Dan Rodelo backed off a step, then did an about-face and walked out of the office. He was tight inside with apprehension. Did the warden know something? Yet how could he?

Nevertheless . . .

The guard who walked beside him signaled for the gate to be opened as they approached it. They paused there briefly.

"I'm glad to see you out of here, Dan," the guard said.

"Thanks, Turkey. I won't say I'll miss it."

Dan Rodelo nodded his head toward the east. "I've got a good horse waiting for me over there." He turned back. "Want to do something for me?" He took the five-dollar gold piece from his pocket. "This is for you if you'll tell Joe Harbin I gave it to you."

"Is that all?"

"That's all."

Turkey stood in the open gateway watching Rodelo walk down the hill, then he glanced at the gold piece, shrugged, and put it in his pocket. Now what did all that mean? For a moment he considered reporting it to the warden, but on second thought it seemed too trivial. He stepped back and the gates closed behind him.

Thoughtfully, he walked back to the prison yard. Joe Harbin, he knew, would be in the quarry. A prisoner, Turkey was thinking, who could give away five dollars for nothing must be a man who had money—or expected to come into some. And that might be just what he wanted Harbin to know.

IT WAS HOT.

Dan Rodelo paused and wiped his hand across his forehead. It was going to be a long walk to the ghost mining town toward which he was headed, and he would be better off to wait until after sundown. He wanted to avoid Yuma, with its curious stares for anyone who came down the hill from the Territorial Prison. It had been a year since they had seen him, and only a glimpse then. He wanted no one remembering him in future years as a man who had done time in Yuma.

He turned off the road and came to the shade of an abandoned adobe, where he sat down to wait for the coolness of the evening. Taking his six-shooter from its holster, he tried the balance of it and checked the loads. The cartridge belt held only eleven loops that were carrying shells. He would need ammunition, and he would need a rifle.

He holstered his pistol and, tilting his hat over his

eyes, settled back to rest. It was very hot, but there was a faint breeze from off the river.

As he dozed he remembered the Yaqui in the beat-up old cavalry hat, and for a moment felt a twinge of chill. What was it they said caused that? It was when somebody stepped on your grave.

CHAPTER 2

THE PRISON ROCK quarry was like an oven. Tom Badger turned the drill for Joe Harbin, who swung the double-jack. It was a heavy sledge hammer, and he swung it viciously, without the easy rhythm of a practiced driller.

"Take it easy, you damn fool!" Badger said irritably. "You miss that drill and I might lose a hand."

Badger was squatted at the drill in such a way that he could keep an eye on Perryman, their guard. Tom Badger was an old hand at both rock drilling and prisons, and he knew that a prisoner could not choose his cell mates, nor even those he would include in an escape. Circumstances did that for you, and then you made the best of it.

"I'm doin' life," Harbin said, "and that damn Rodelo walkin' out—just one year! I could do that standin' on my head."

"You killed a man to get that payroll."

Joe Harbin took a fresh grip on the handle of the double-jack. His anger was suddenly gone, and in its place was a cold, careful calculation. "What payroll?"

Badger turned the drill. "That mine payroll. Fifty thousand dollars in gold."

"You talk too much."

"It burns you to see Dan walk out of here and pick up that loot," Badger said.

"He don't know where I hid it."

"He's got a good idea. He told me so. He said when his time was nearly up you'd try to break out and beat him to it, and that's exactly what you did."

"What about you?" Harbin said roughly. "You didn't make it either."

Badger spat on the ground suddenly, the signal that the guard was turning. Harbin swung the heavy sledge, gathered it and swung again. When the guard had turned back to the other convicts, Badger said quietly, "My break failed when I tried to go it alone. Yours failed because you weren't smart, but if we had been partners . . ."

They worked in silence. Finally, Harbin said grudgingly, "You got any ideas?"

"Uh-huh . . . I've got several, and I can make them work, but I need a partner."

"I'd like to get down to Mexico," Harbin muttered. "I like them Mexican women."

"We could pick up that payroll, split it two ways, and—"

"Split? You crazy? D'you think I stood up that payroll to split it with somebody?"

"We'd be partners."

Joe started to speak again and Tom Badger spat swiftly into the dirt, but Harbin, too irritated to think, spoke out angrily. "Yeah? You think—"

Perryman was suddenly beside them. "There'll be no talking here!"

Harbin turned on him, ugly with rage. "You—!"

Perryman's reaction was swift. He had handled too many tough cons and he knew what was coming. The butt stroke with his rifle was chopping, vicious, and it caught Harbin coming in. He was knocked to his knees, blood flowing from a split scalp.

Backing off, Perryman looked at Badger. "What about you?"

"We were havin' an argument, Perryman. Don't blame Joe—the heat got him."

Perryman hesitated, but Tom Badger was smiling deprecatingly. "Joe's feelin' the heat. He's Montana-born, y' know, and can't take it like you an' me."

Mollified, Perryman stepped back. "All right. I'll make no report on him this time. But if you're a friend of his, you keep him in line, d'you hear?" He mopped his forehead. "It is hot, damn it! I can't scarcely blame him."

He walked away, and Badger helped Harbin to his feet. The blood was not much more than a trickle, but Harbin was still glassy-eyed. "You saved my bacon," he said.

"Why not? Ain't we partners?"

Harbin still hesitated. "What about those ideas you got?"

"I can put you in Mazatlan . . . with that gold . . . in ten days."

"All right—partner."

"Here," Badger held out the drill. "You turn the drill. And by all that's holy, don't get that guard sore. If they separate us now, I'll go out of here alone."

Joe Harbin settled down glumly to his work. All right, if that was what it took, that was what he would do. He would work so hard they would pay no more attention to him. His head was throbbing, but he had been knocked down before, and always within him was the thought of the money that awaited, and of beating Rodelo to the cache.

When Turkey came up he scarcely saw him, or even realized his presence until the guard spoke. "Don't you ever get tired, Joe?"

"Not me."

"Your friend Rodelo signed out this morning. Look what he gave me." He showed them the gold coin, watching their expressions. There was something behind all this, Turkey felt sure, and he was curious. "This was his eating money until he found himself a job. I can't figure that man."

When Harbin offered no comment, Turkey walked away, and Badger took over holding the drill on the new hole. "If Dan doesn't need that money," he said, "he must have a good idea where he can get more."

"I got to get out of here." Harbin's eyes were wild. "Tom, we got to get out."

"We'll get out. We'll get out tonight."

Harbin's head jerked up in astonishment. "Tonight?"

"You be ready. About sundown."

Joe Harbin's tongue touched his lips, and he glanced at the sun . . . a couple of hours to go. He could feel cold sweat inside his shirt. Was he scared? Well . . . maybe. But he was going through with it, no matter what. He could already taste that cold Mexican beer . . . or the tequila. Now, there was a drink!

As they worked, the sun's heat was thrown back by the sandstone, and it was fierce, blistering, turning the bottom of the quarry into an oven. The careless touch of an ungloved hand to a steel drill would sear the flesh, and across the quarry two men had dropped from the heat, but Joe Harbin continued to work steadily. Tom Badger, a slower, more methodical worker, nevertheless accomplished as much. Badger had no lost motion, no wasted effort. He had worked enough to know all the knacks and tricks that made hard work easier.

Miller, the nearest guard toward the end of the long, blistering afternoon, walked down to them. They were completing the last hole of their round, well ahead of any of the others.

"You fellows outworked every team on the job. Go turn in your tools. You've done enough for today."

Badger straightened up, rubbing his back. "Thanks, sir. I guess you're right. We'd best save something for tomorrow."

Badger picked up the drills one by one while Joe Harbin shouldered the double-jack. During a moment when the guard's attention was distracted, Badger kicked one drill away among the rocks, then slowly the two walked off. Glancing back, Badger saw the powder-monkey was already dropping sticks of giant powder into the drilled holes, tamping them home with a long stick.

Badger's eyes swept the quarry, measuring distances, imagining the scene as it would be, and carefully estimating his chances. For a moment his eyes held on Gopher, who was struggling with a heavy wheelbarrow loaded with broken rock. The boy looked bad . . . he would never live out his term, Badger thought.

Turning, he walked on beside Harbin toward the prison tool shed, where a trusty was checking the tools as they were brought in.

"You're early tonight. Miller must be goin' soft," the man said. He grinned at Badger. "All right, Harbin. You got your hammer?"

Joe Harbin placed the double-jack on the shelf at the door, inadvertently glancing over his shoulder. His mouth was dry and he was jumpy, knowing that any minute now—

Badger had swung his drills to the shelf and the trusty glanced over at them. "You're a drill short, Tom."

"I must've overlooked it," Badger said calmly. "I was in a hurry to get in."

"Well, you hustle right back there and find it. You know the rules."

Badger walked back slowly, timing each step, knowing eyes were on him. He also knew that when he bent to pick up the drill he would be momentarily out of sight of the guard, now standing over the prisoners lower down in the quarry, and of the trusty in the tool shed.

As he stepped down, apparently searching for the drill, he suddenly dropped to one knee, struck a wooden match hoarded for the purpose and lighted the newly placed fuse, then another, and another. He picked up the drill and walked slowly away.

He knew how long it would take for the fuse to burn, knew when the explosion would come, and knew what must follow if there was to be an escape. Tom Badger was a careful man and he had planned every move with care, yet even as he planned there had lurked in his mind the shadow of the Yaquis. There was no way to plan for them, or to make plans against them. It came down to a simple matter of outrunning them if possible, or outfighting them if it was not.

He came up to the tool shed. "Here's your drill. Satisfied?"

"It ain't me, Tom," the trusty said. "It's the rules. You got to abide by them."

As he reached to take the drill from Badger's hand the air was suddenly torn by a shattering blast, and in the instant of the explosion Badger swung the steel drill and struck the trusty on the skull.

The sound of the explosion died amid a burst of yells, and then came screams of pain from the injured, guards and convicts alike. Instantly, Tom and Harbin ran toward the quarry. The first body they came upon was that of Perryman, half covered with rocks and sand. Jerking the body free, Badger ripped the gun belt and pistol from the guard's hips, shucking the cartridges swiftly into his palm from the belt, then thrusting the gun into his pants.

Seizing the rifle of the fallen guard, Joe Harbin smashed it against a rock.

Convicts and guards were struggling to crawl out of the welter of smoke, dust, and debris. Several staggered up, bleeding, and started to clamber out of the quarry. Pushing past them, Badger climbed out of the quarry and ran toward the team and wagon that stood nearby.

The warden suddenly appeared, accompanied by several guards. He paused abruptly, staring down at the confusion in the quarry, while the guards ran on down the ramp to give aid to those below.

Tom Badger moved quickly to the warden's side, thrusting the gun into his ribs. Harbin closed in on the other side, jerking the warden's pistol from its holster.

"We got nothin' against you, warden, so if you want to go on livin' just head for that wagon."

"I'll do—"

"Warden," Badger warned, "we ain't got time to argue. You head for the wagon."

The warden started to protest and Harbin promptly slammed him over the head with a gun barrel. Quickly, they dragged him to the wagon and heaved him in. Tom

Badger caught up the reins and the team started for the gate at a smart trot.

Joe Harbin pulled the warden in front of him and propped him up so he could be seen. The plan was working! Now, if only—

"Halt!"

Badger kept the wagon moving forward, and a second guard stepped out of the watch tower beside the gate, with shotgun lifted. "Halt, or we fire!"

"Open that gate," Badger ordered, "or you'll have a dead warden on your hands."

Hesitating, the guards glanced right and left, looking for help, but there was none. The deputy warden and the others had rushed to aid the injured in the quarry.

"You've got three seconds," Harbin said, "and then I blow the warden's head off and we shoot it out. . . . One!"

The guards looked at each other. They owed their jobs to the warden, who was a friendly, pleasant man, although stern where duty was concerned.

"Two!"

One of the guards turned sharply and went to the rope that opened the gate. Without a word he began hauling on the rope. The gate opened . . . all too slowly. Joe Harbin could feel the sweat trying to find a way through his thick eyebrows, and he could feel the hair crawling on the back of his neck. At any moment there would be shooting.

Then the gate was open and they went through, walking the horse until the wagon was safely clear, then picking up the team to a fast trot.

They were at the break of the hill. "Drop him!" Tom said, and Joe Harbin shoved the still unconscious warden from the wagon and Tom Badger slapped the horses with a whip. Instantly they broke into a run. From the tower at the gate came a rifle shot, another, and then they were shielded by the break of the hill.

Suddenly from behind them the bell began to peal, and Badger swung the wagon off the road and into the brush at the base of the hill. They moved along through the brush, bumping over stones, but holding to a good pace.

A dry wash suddenly showed and Badger turned into it, the wagon making no sound in the soft sand. They drove on around the bend, then Badger said, "Beyond that rock cut the team loose and mount up. Here!" He tossed Harbin a hackamore that he took from inside his shirt.

Swiftly, they stripped the harness from the two horses and, slipping the hackamores on, they mounted up, bareback. They rode south, holding to the soft sand where the hoofs of the horses left no definite prints, merely indentations in the loose soil.

From the wash they rode into the bottoms and went a devious route through the acres of willows growing near the river. Suddenly Badger turned sharply and left the willows, riding again into the drift sand of the dunes.

Joe Harbin, following a horse's length behind, could only admire. It was obvious that Tom Badger had planned every bit of this. He had entered the willows where no tracks would be left, and now he left them at a place where tracking would be equally difficult.

Badger kept glancing at the sky, and for the first time Harbin thought of the hour. That, too was well chosen. It would be sundown in a matter of minutes, and dark soon after, as always in desert country. Then they could ride on, comparatively secure until dawn.

But Joe Harbin was a suspicious man. Badger had planned well, every step of the way . . . what plans did he have for the time after they got the gold? It was an unpleasant thought, but Joe Harbin had been doing his own thinking along those lines and he was wondering just how far he wanted to go with Badger.

The trouble was they needed that boat, and Harbin was not at all sure how the crew of the boat could be handled. He was sure that Badger had a plan for that too, and Harbin might need him to help. Moreover, if the Yaquis came after them each of them would need the other to help. Standing off desert-wise Yaquis would be no simple task.

Among the sand dunes, Badger drew up and waited for Harbin to come alongside.

"You tell me straight, Joe, and no hedging. Does anybody know where that gold is hidden?"

"You think I'm crazy? Nobody knows."

Badger considered that. If nobody knew, it was unlikely that either the Yaquis or the warden would guess their direction, for despite their need to get away they would be riding east rather than south . . . at least until they found the gold.

But if anybody knew, and if the warden was tipped off, he could be in the vicinity of the gold, watching for them. In that case they might as well throw in their hand.

"If you're lyin'," Badger said, "it'll be your neck as well as mine. If one person other than you knows where that gold is, or even knows about where it is, then you can lay a bet somebody else knows, and we'll be walkin' into a trap."

"Nobody knows," Harbin said shortly.

Only somebody did know, Harbin was thinking. That girl knew . . . he had talked big, talked when he should have been listening.

Hell, what did that matter? She was probably long gone out of the country.

CHAPTER 3

WHEN THE SUN was still half an hour above the horizon, Dan Rodelo took the trail. He had always enjoyed walking, something rare among riding men, and he enjoyed it now. After a year in prison it was a grand feeling to be out on the open road, swinging along at a good gait. Above all, it gave him time to think, and to plan.

It was not yet dark when he heard the rattle of a light wagon behind him, and turned to see a four-horse team approaching, drawing a light wagon with a saddle horse tied behind. In the wagon were two men and a woman.

When they came abreast of him, they drew up. "You goin' some place, mister?"

"Gold City."

"If you're huntin' gold it's no place to go. The only gold they ever found there was in the name."

"I might be lucky."

"Get in. We're goin' thataway." The big man spoke to the team, slapped them lightly with the reins, and the wagon rolled off with Rodelo in the back, sitting near a girl, and a damned attractive one, he decided.

"That's a ghost town now, mister. You realize that?"

"It's not quite a ghost town. Old Sam Burrows is still around. He runs the store and saloon. I left my horse with him some time back."

"Seems a far-off place to leave a horse," the big man commented.

"Does, doesn't it?"

Dan Rodelo looked at the girl, who regarded him coolly, showing no interest. The two men exchanged comments from time to time, and Rodelo gathered their names were Clint and Jake.

The night was still, and when the horses slowed to walk up a long hill, there was no sound to be heard but that of their own passage. Dan Rodelo stretched out his legs. It felt good to be riding. He eased his holster into a handy position and caught the girl's glance as she noticed it.

They were wondering about him, as he was about them. Two men and a girl going to Gold City . . . for what?

Gold City was not only a ghost town, but it was the end of the trail. Beyond lay the desert . . . a desert that was empty all the way to the border, and far beyond. Dan Rodelo was not really a suspicious man, but at the moment he was wondering if somebody else had the same idea he had. It would be wise to be careful, very careful.

Gold City was not much more than a ramshackle store and saloon, three steps up from the walk to the porch under the overhang. Across the street stood an adobe, crumbling to ruin, and there was a scattering of other abandoned buildings along this street and back from it on both sides. There was no tree in sight, nothing but creosote brush, brittle bush, and a scattering of prickly pear and ocotillo.

Sam, smoking his pipe on the porch, watched the

wagon approach. The dog lying at his feet growled, then subsided. Sam wore a belt gun, which he could use, and there was a shotgun just inside the door.

As the wagon rolled to a halt his wary old eyes slid over the occupants, then held on Rodelo.

"Hiya, Sam!"

"Bless my soul, if it ain't Rodelo. I'd no idea your time was up."

Dan dropped to the ground. "These strangers gave me a lift. Mighty kind of them."

He had underlined the word "strangers" just a little, and Sam understood. He glanced at them, smiling. "Reckon you boys could do with a bit of something."

"You got some whiskey?" Jake asked.

"Best in town," Sam said. He struggled to his feet and lumbered through the door ahead of them. "Can't say I've got much competition."

Placing two glasses and a bottle before them, he then glanced at the girl. "And you, ma'am, a spot of coffee?"

"Show me where it is and I'll make it."

"Right through the door, ma'am. You'll find everything easy to hand."

"You carry quite a stock for a ghost town," the man called Clint commented.

"We ain't as lonesome here as a body would think. Lots of cattlemen, and sometimes there's one of them Arizona Rangers or some Wells Fargo man . . . prospectors too, and the like of that."

"I didn't think there was anything between here and the Gulf."

"There ain't. Port Isabel down there ships some beef

stock. That's about it." He nodded his head toward the desert. "Most God-forsaken country on earth."

Sam refilled the glasses. "Have one on the house. Always like comp'ny, and any friend of Dan's is a friend of mine." He glanced at them, his eyes innocent. "Plenty of accommodation in this town, such as it is. Where you from, mister?"

"Flagstaff," Clint replied.

Jake shifted his weight and glanced irritably at Clint.

"Ain't much worth seein' down here unless you're prospectin'," Sam said.

"Anything wrong with that?"

"You know your own business."

"That we do, old-timer." Jake tossed off his drink. "Let's go, Clint," he said.

"You ain't had your coffee yet."

"That was for Nora—Nora Paxton. If she wants coffee, let her have it. I want to find a place to bed down."

"I'd better see if the lady needs help." Sam turned toward the door at the back of the bar but Jake stepped in front of him. "I'll do that, mister."

Dan Rodelo sat very still. He had found a kitchen chair near the other end of the bar and had seated himself, keeping out of the way, but with everything within range of his vision. He could hear the faint murmur of voices from the kitchen but he could not distinguish what they were saying.

Nora was standing by the stove when Jake Andrews entered. "We're goin' to look around and find that 'dobe," he said. "We don't want anybody over that way, d'you hear?"

"I'll do what I can."

"Just be damn sure you don't do too much. I don't know who that man is, but I don't like him. And he's fresh out of Yuma."

Nora Paxton looked at him sharply. "That's where Joe Harbin is!"

"You're right. How do we know this gent ain't a friend of Joe's? You be careful."

As Jake went out she filled a cup, and took the cup and the coffee pot into the other room.

Dan Rodelo was on his feet. She looked at him, seeing him in the light for the first time; she had not dared to notice him while Jake Andrews and Clint Wilson were near.

He was tall, a wide-shouldered, easy-moving young man with a dark, lean face and high cheekbones. He was well dressed for a man just out of prison, so they must be clothes he had when he went in.

"I'd better be findin' a place to bed down myself," Rodelo said.

"So soon? The party is just beginning," Nora said.

"What party?"

"The one we're going to have." She put the cup down in front of him, and placed the pot on the table. "I'll get some more cups." Turning, she saw the guitar on the shelf. "Do you play that, Sam?"

"A mite . . . when I'm by myself. Dan here, he used to play almighty well. How about it, Dan?"

"Not now," said Rodelo.

Outside in the street Clint had walked to the wagon and picked up a lantern, raised the globe, and struck a match to the wick. The first match went out, the second caught, and he lowered the globe in place.

Jake came up to him. "Down that way, I'm thinkin'," he said.

They walked away together, lifting the lantern to look at the houses on the other side of the street. Finally they saw the adobe they were looking for, the door standing a few inches ajar. Over the door was a horseshoe that had been nailed in place with the front of the shoe at the bottom, but the nails at the top had come out and the shoe had fallen so that the open part at the back of the shoe pointed toward the ground.

Jake hesitated, not liking the looks of it. "Clint, look at that. The luck's run out. When a shoe hangs that way the luck runs out the bottom."

"What do we care? It ain't our 'dobe, so it ain't our luck. No tellin' what happened to the man who nailed that shoe up there."

"Maybe it's a sign. Maybe our luck *has* run out."

"Don't be a damn fool."

Clint pushed by him and went into the room. It was a simple, whitewashed room with a fireplace, its only furniture a rough table, two chairs, and two bunks against the far wall. Clint found a chain hook hanging from the center beam and hung the lantern on it.

"Now we're alone with fifty thousand dollars."

"But where is it?"

"That's up to us. You can't get more out of folks than they know . . . an adobe on this street with a horseshoe over the door."

"Women! First it was Harbin's girl, and now this Paxton girl you insisted on bringin' along."

"Leave Nora out of it. She's decent."

"All right, she's out of it. But now, where's the gold?"

Jake Andrews looked around the room, and studied the floor. Treasure is buried, as a rule, he knew. He examined the floor more carefully. It was pieced together of odds and ends of planks, only a few of which ran the full length of the floor, and none of them seemed in any way special. Obviously, the floor had been put in after the adobe had been built, and the pieces of board had been taken from older buildings.

"He had to leave some mark," Jake said. "Now, what would it be?"

"You're forgettin', friend. He *knew* where he buried it."

"Just the same, he wouldn't chance it. He'd know that time and dust and wear change the looks of things. He didn't figure that gold would be left here long, but he knew he wouldn't be taking it up the next day. You can bet he left some kind of a marker."

The whitewash on the walls was very old but it looked undisturbed. It seemed unlikely that anything could have been hidden there without leaving some indication. The fireplace, too, had not been disturbed, so far as they could see. Jake went back to examining the floor. Squatting on his haunches, he studied it section by section.

"Clint!" he exclaimed suddenly. "Look!"

He pointed at one section of a board, but it was a moment or so before Clint could see what it was Jake was pointing at. Then he saw it—a crude arrow of rusted nail heads.

The nails were driven in to fasten the board in place but there was a line of more nails than necessary, and then two extra nails had been placed so as to make a crude arrow. Was it just accident? Or was this the clue they were looking for?

"Let's rip it out of there." Jake looked about, then went back to the door with the lantern. "Seems to me I saw a pick outside the door," he said.

Clint waited, staring at the plank. It was there, then. Fifty thousand dollars . . . a man could do a lot with that amount.

Jake came back and put the lantern down. "Just the pick, no handle," he said.

Thrusting the flat end into the crack between the boards, he pulled back. The rusty nails gave easily in the worn board. A second tug on the pick and the board came loose, splintering around the nails.

Eagerly, Clint grasped the board and ripped it away. Under the floor was a wooden box bound with iron straps.

"That's it!" Jake said. "Fifty thousand dollars!"

"Yeah," Clint said flatly. "I got it made."

Jake looked up inquiringly. His expression changed slowly. Clint held a gun in his hand. "Clint! You—"

The gun muzzle stabbed flame, the shot thundered in the empty old adobe, then sounded again. Jake Andrews sagged forward, his mouth opening as if to speak.

Clint holstered his gun and, kneeling, dragged the box up through the hole he had ripped in the floor. With the pick he broke open the box, smashing the still solid wood, then he swore.

The box was packed with old letters, deeds, assay reports, and a variety of legal papers. Reaching in with both hands, he brought out a double handful and spilled them on the floor. There was no sign of any money. Desperately, he went to the bottom of the box, scratching about with both hands . . . nothing.

Up the street he heard a door slam, and there was a sound of running feet.

Springing up, he looked wildly around, then ran to the door and peered out. Dan Rodelo was coming down the street toward him, with Nora close behind.

Instantly, he lifted his gun and fired, aware even as he pulled the trigger that he had shot too quickly and had missed.

Dan ducked across the street and into the deeper shadows, calling to Nora as he did so. "Get out of the light! He'll kill you!"

Clint leaned from the door, caught a glimpse of Nora's moving figure and threw his gun into position. Catching the glint of light on the gun barrel, Dan fired. Clint's gun dropped and he disappeared into the building. Swiftly, Rodelo crossed the street, gun ready.

Clint ran to Jake's body, toed him over, and grabbed at the dead man's gun with his good hand.

"Drop it!" Rodelo was in the doorway. "I don't want to kill you."

Nora, staring at Jake's body, suddenly lifted her eyes to Clint. "You killed him. *You!*"

Snatching Jake's gun, she lifted it, but before she could fire, Dan wrenched the gun from her hand.

"I might need him, Nora."

"You," he motioned at Clint with the gun. "Get into that bunk."

"What's the idea?"

"We'll be waiting for a while. Better make yourself comfortable."

"What about my hand?"

Rodelo glanced at the hand, which was bloody but did not appear to have been more than creased. "Wrap it up. You won't lose much blood." He gestured toward the dead man. "You're better off than he is."

"Why don't you shoot him?" Nora said. "He tried to kill you."

"I'm not the law, nor am I justice. But if he shoots at me again I will kill him."

"What became of Sam Burrows?" Nora asked. "He didn't even come out on the street."

"Why should he? Sam's lived a long time by minding his own business."

Gathering up the guns, Rodelo tucked the spares behind his belt. He had an idea that before the night was over he might need all the fire power he could get.

"I'm going back to finish that coffee," Nora said finally.

He looked at her thoughtfully. "Go ahead. And take your time."

Then there was silence in the room. The lantern lit the room only dimly, and Clint lay on his back, nursing his wounded wrist and thinking. Dan Rodelo had no doubts as to what he was thinking and he knew that, given a chance, Clint would kill him even as he had killed his partner.

The trouble for Clint was that he had no idea what to do. He wanted the gold, and it must be somewhere about; but when he believed the gold had been found he had killed the one man who might have known. There might even be a clue in that mass of papers, but in which one? What kind of a clue?

Rodelo, as he waited, was trying to think from Clint's viewpoint. The man wanted to kill him, but he would not be likely to take a chance until he had some clue to the gold, or had the gold itself.

Hearing footsteps, Rodelo looked out. It was Nora, carrying the coffee pot and some cups.

"Sam said to bring it along, you might need it." She placed a cup on the table and filled it for Rodelo, then one for Clint and one for herself.

Dan took his time about picking up the cup, allowing Clint and Nora to take theirs first. Noticing this, Nora said, "Don't you trust me?"

He grinned at her. "Not when there's fifty thousand dollars in the pot."

She sipped some of the coffee, and he smiled and did the same. "You make a mighty good cup of coffee," he commented, "and there's nothing better."

He listened to the night, alert for strange sounds. They would come, he was sure of that. Though how could he be sure? They had been locked up in Yuma prison when he left, but men had escaped from Yuma before, and if anyone could do it, Tom Badger could and would.

His waiting, his listening seemed to taunt the two with him. It was deliberate, for he was hoping to get a move from them at once. He had to locate that gold.

"You're expecting someone?" Nora asked.

He nodded. "That I am. I'm expecting the men who buried that gold."

Clint turned his head around sharply, half rising.

"But they're in Yuma prison!" Nora objected.

"I'm gambling they'll be here before daybreak," Rodelo said calmly. "There was a bit of a ruckus at the prison before I got out of town. I'm betting it was them."

Clint sat up. "They'll kill us all!" he exclaimed. "Every one of us!"

"Maybe . . . maybe not."

CHAPTER 4

TOM BADGER DREW up and swung his horse off the trail. "Get out of sight, Joe. Somebody's comin'."

Harbin swung over, drawing his gun. "It can't be anybody I want to see, and there's nobody we want to see us."

The horse was coming at a good gait, then it slowed, and drew up opposite them. The rider was standing in his stirrups, apparently listening.

"Must've turned off," the rider said, "I don't hear 'em." He spoke aloud to himself, as many lonely men do.

"Hell!" Harbin was exasperated. "It's Gopher!"

They rode out to meet him, Tom Badger with considerably more irritation than Harbin. Their own trail was, he was sure, lost back there by the river, and the Yaquis would be trailing south, hunting them. Gopher would know nothing about not leaving a trail and might have been followed right to this point. If so, all their efforts had gone for nothing.

"You fellers gave me a chance," Gopher said. "When you made a break everybody got all excited an' everybody was tryin' to catch you. Three of us made a break. I figure the other two got shot."

"Let's get on with it," Badger said impatiently. "Rodelo will have been there and gone before we get to Gold City."

The night held no sound but the creak of their saddles. Tom Badger led off, walking his horse slowly until it was safely in the dust of the trail, then he put the animal to a canter and the others followed.

Gopher was a problem, but that could be taken care of, if it did not take care of itself. Gopher had been lucky to escape, for he was particularly inept; but he could not be lucky all the time, and the days ahead would leave no margin for luck.

When they came to Gold City, they walked their horses down the street. A light glowed from the store, but they did not stop. Down the street they saw that there was a light in the adobe as well.

"He's got here first," Badger said.

"He's in the adobe," said Harbin. "That don't say he's found my stuff. Nobody will find it but me."

"Probably grabbed it and pulled out," Gopher said.

"And leave the shack all lit up?"

Joe Harbin walked his horse up beside the nearest building to the adobe, then swung down, and drew his gun.

Inside the adobe, Dan Rodelo waited, his face calm. Nora had drawn back into a corner out of range of gunfire. Clint watched from the edge of the bunk. "There's more than one man out there," he said. "You goin' to tackle them alone?"

"Uh-huh."

"You're a fool." Clint looked at him. "What do I get out of this?"

"You bought in. You killed your partner. You can sit right there, or you can gamble and run for it. You might get away."

"I'll stay right here."

"You do that. Joe Harbin's out there."

"So?"

"The only way you could know about this gold is through his woman. And Joe's a mighty jealous man."

"It wasn't me!" Clint protested. "It was Jake."

"You tell him that. Maybe he'll listen."

From out in front there was a sound of a boot scraping on stone, and then a voice called, "Hey, Danny! Come on out!"

"Well, there they are, Clint," Rodelo said. "You sit right there and they'll figure you're in this with me."

Clint got up suddenly. "I want out. I want to get out of here right now."

"Go ahead."

Clint started toward the door, then hesitated. "How about a gun?"

Dan Rodelo drew a pistol from his belt and handed it to Clint, barrel first. "Now face the door. If you turn around I'll shoot."

Clint took the gun and stepped toward the door. Then he called, "This ain't Danny! I want to come out—I want to talk!"

Dan Rodelo was at the back door, easing up on the latch.

"All right," Joe Harbin's voice came clear. "Come out with your hands up."

Clint opened the door, gun in hand, stepped quickly outside, and fired. Three guns cut him down before he got off a second shot.

"You stay there," Rodelo whispered to Nora, and like a shadow he was gone into the night.

Gopher stepped through the door and paused, peering at the body on the floor. He came on into the room and was followed by Harbin and Badger.

Tom Badger looked slowly around the room, stared at Nora, then at the body on the floor. "Turn him over," he told Gopher.

The convict knelt and turned Jake's body over. "It ain't Danny," he said, surprised.

"That's Jake Andrews," Harbin commented. "And that was Clint Wilson we killed."

"Clint *Wilson*?"

"The same," Harbin replied grimly. He looked over at Nora. "And whose little girl are you?"

"I was with those men . . . I am nobody's girl. I am Nora Paxton."

"Let's get what we came for," Tom said impatiently. "Joe, get your mind off women. There's plenty of them in Mexico."

"You were with them?" Joe persisted.

"They were going down to the Gulf, and that was where I wanted to go. They offered to take me along, and there was no other way."

"The Gulf? Why the Gulf?"

"Business . . . *my* business, and none of yours."

Harbin grinned at her. "No offense, ma'am. If you still want to go, you can go with us."

Badger was looking at her now. "How did they expect to make it to the Gulf?"

"They had a wagon up the street, and they were going to Papago Wells."

"And then?"

"I know where there is a water hole between there and the Gulf. That's one reason they wanted me along."

"I never heard of any such water hole," Badger said.

"It's there . . . a good pool of permanent water, sweet water."

"If that's true," Joe said, "our troubles are over. Okay, you can come along."

Badger looked at the box and the scattered papers. "I don't see any gold. You sure Rodelo didn't get it and light out?"

"Was he the man who was just here? The tall, dark young man?"

"That's our Danny."

"He had nothing when he left here." Then she added, "Clint shot Jake. He thought they'd found the gold when Jake located that box, so he just killed him."

"Ain't the first time . . . not for Clint."

Nora was listening. Was Dan Rodelo outside? What was he planning?

"Get the gold," Badger said. "Let's get out of here!"

Harbin took a rusted poker from the fireplace and pulled a chair over to a place under the central beam that crossed the room from wall to wall. Standing on the chair, he inserted the end of the poker into what looked like a crack, then pried up. A crudely cut piece of beam lifted up, revealing a compartment within the heavy beam itself. As he lifted this a gold piece fell to the floor. Nora picked it up and handed it to Badger. "It's gold, all right," she said.

Harbin grinned his triumph. "You're darned tootin', it is! And there's plenty of it, baby."

Badger turned to Gopher. "Get the saddlebags. Quick, now!"

When he had gone out, Harbin said, "What about him?"

Badger shrugged. "We can use help on the trip. When we get to Mazatlan, give him fifty bucks and send him packin'."

Gopher came back carrying two pairs of saddlebags, and swiftly they began loading the gold into them. "This is going to be heavy," Tom commented thoughtfully. "I wish we had an extra horse or two."

Dan Rodelo, moving quietly, had come in the front door. He held a gun in his right hand, and once inside he moved out of the doorway and stood a moment watching. Tom Badger saw him first, and slowly, carefully, he lifted his hands. He had never seen Dan Rodelo shoot, but he had an idea he would be good.

"That's all of it," Harbin said.

"Let me look," Gopher pleaded.

"Go ahead."

Gopher got up on the table and ran his hand back into the opening, feeling around. "Got it!" he yelled, and withdrew his hand, hitting it against the edge in his excitement. "Two of them."

"Keep 'em," Harbin said. "That will be your part of this."

"You mean that's all I get?"

"You're out of prison, ain't you?"

"Big-hearted Joe Harbin! You were always a generous man, Joe." Dan Rodelo spoke softly, and Joe Harbin's hand opened slightly as though for a draw.

"Don't try it, Joe."

Slowly, Harbin's hands went up, as did Gopher's. Joe turned carefully, grinning at Rodelo. "How are you,

Danny? You don't need that gun with me. We're friends, remember?"

Rodelo smiled. Harbin had never liked him, and he knew it. "Then you will not object if I cut myself in for part of this?"

"You're talkin' crazy. I did this job all by myself, and you know it."

"And I did time for it."

"Let's get out of here!" Badger interrupted. "We'll have the law all around us if we don't, and then there won't be anything for anybody."

Picking up one set of the saddlebags, he turned toward the door. "Come on. We'll get their wagon and trail our horses behind."

Dan Rodelo did not move. "How do you figure on going?"

"South . . . why?"

"It'll be the wrong way. Go east from here first, then down the eastern side of the Gilas. By the time they've covered everything else you'll be on board that boat down on the Gulf."

They stared at him, their eyes hard with suspicion. "What are you talkin' about? What boat?" Harbin said.

Dan Rodelo motioned with his gun barrel. "Get loaded up. You're right, Badger, time's running out. You made a mistake when you hit the warden. He's a good man, but a hard man when you push him, and you pushed too hard."

"What's that mean?" Harbin demanded.

"He won't quit, not even a little bit. You've got to run faster and farther than you ever did before. The warden, you know, used to be an army officer, and he has friends along the Mexican border that he helped during the Apache troubles. He'll have them hunting you, too."

Swiftly, they carried the loot out to the horse and, motioning Nora ahead of him, Dan Rodelo followed. Gopher carried the lantern.

Mounting up, they rode back to the store and went to the wagon Jake and Clint had driven to Gold City.

"What about him?" Harbin gestured toward the store.

"Forget about him," Rodelo said. "He knows every man on the dodge from here to El Paso, and he's never opened his mouth yet. Sam Burrows is a good man to have on your side, but if he got hurt you'd be ducking the outlaws as well as the law."

"There's water in the wagon," Nora said. "We filled up some cans and water sacks before we started."

"We'll want more," Rodelo said. He turned to Gopher, reaching into the sack for a gold piece as he did so. "Take this and buy every water sack or canteen in the store. Then we'll fill 'em. That's a long trek without water."

The desert's heat had not yet gone from the air, and there was no breeze now. Only the stars hanging low in the sky above them seemed cool. It was still, very still. Dan Rodelo stood at one side and watched them prepare. He watched the sacks and canteens filled; every one of them would be needed for the hell that lay to the south. There were water holes and tanks between them and the border, and perhaps beyond the border, too, but he knew only too well, and better than anyone here, how uncertain such desert tanks can be.

He tried to remember when it had rained last, but it does not rain often in Yuma, and many rains in these parts were local. That desert to the south was pure hell, but more than that, nobody had taken a wagon the way he intended to take them. Well, they would find that out in due time.

At the end he went inside. "Thanks, Sam," he said. "It's good to have my horse again."

"That *grulla* is quite a horse," Sam said. "I almost wished you didn't come back."

"He came from this country, Sam. South of here. He was a bronco two-year-old when I put a rope on him. When the going gets rough down south, I'm going to need that horse. He knows all the water holes in Sonora, I think."

Sam put his palms flat on the bar and leaned toward him. "You're runnin' a long chance, boy. You sure you don't want help? There's some I could send—"

"It's my job, and I'll do it."

"Joe Harbin," Sam said, "has killed eleven men I know of . . . in stand-up gun battles."

"Yeah." Rodelo was serious for a moment. "But the one who really worries me is Badger. He's cunning as a prairie wolf."

"Comes by it natural. His pa was a half-breed, and he raised his youngsters mean." Sam paused. "That girl, now. She doesn't seem like their sort. I can't make her out."

"No." Rodelo hesitated. "If I can, I'll get them to leave her with you."

"I could put her on the stage. Buy her a ticket either way she wants to go."

Dan Rodelo started toward the door, then paused. "Put out the light, Sam."

Only when the room was dark did he walk to the door and step out.

"You sure don't trust a feller," Harbin said.

Dan went toward them. "I trust you, Joe. I just don't want you to have too much trouble with your conscience, that's all."

He stopped near them. "What about this girl? That's a rough trip ahead. Why don't we leave her here?"

"You're crazy! She's seen the gold, heard us talk. We can't leave her now."

"It's up to you, Joe."

Harbin turned his head. His eyes were black holes in the darkness under his hat brim. "Why me?"

"You're the killer in this outfit."

"Me? Shoot a woman?"

"We're wasting time," Nora said quietly. "Joe wouldn't shoot me, and neither would the rest of you. Let's go . . . and save your ammunition for those Yaquis or Yumas or whatever they are."

Dan Rodelo took the reins and turned the wagon into the road, their horses following behind on lead ropes. He drove slowly at first, then at a swinging trot until they reached the road east. He slowed down then, letting the horses take their time, and after a bit he brought them to a trot once more. In the back of the wagon Badger stretched out beside Harbin to sleep. Gopher curled up against the tailgate.

"I don't understand you," Nora whispered. "What are you doing?"

Rodelo smiled at her. "Beautiful night, isn't it?"

"You might have gotten me killed!"

"Joe Harbin wouldn't kill a woman . . . not without

a good reason—unless he needed your horse, or something."

"And then?"

"He'd kill you, all right. He'd kill you and never give it another thought."

CHAPTER 5

NOW THEY MOVED steadily southward, with the fantastic peaks and ridges of the Gila Mountains on their right. The air was cool and pleasant, and they held to a good pace, stopping at intervals, or after climbing a grade, to rest the horses. Nobody was in any mood for talk. After a while Rodelo gave over the reins to Harbin and turned in, lying stretched out in the back of the wagon.

Presently Badger sat up and lit a cigarette. He glanced over at Rodelo. "You awake?"

Rodelo awakened instantly. "Yeah."

"How far south do these mountains run?"

"To the border."

"Is there a way through them?"

"Uh-huh . . . a couple of ways that I know of. The Indians probably know of others."

Badger considered the matter. "You know this country pretty well?"

"As well as any white man, I expect, but I wouldn't count too much on anything. It's a country with little water, and that hard to find. Folks have died within a few feet of water at Tinajas Altas . . . the water is in rock tanks, high above the trail."

"I've heard of that." Badger was thoughtful. "Do you know of any water down in the Pinacate? She says"—he indicated the sleeping girl—"there's a water hole south and a mite west of Papago Wells."

Dan Rodelo eased the position of his gun to stall for time. Now how in the devil did she know *that*? It was an unlikely place, and he would have gambled that even the Yaquis did not know of it. The Yumas might . . . after all, this was their country, but how did Nora Paxton know of the place?

"Yes," he said reluctantly, "there is such a place. It isn't what I'd call easy to find, but it's there." Then he added, "But you can't depend on any desert water hole to be full all the time. Most of them dry up once in a while, or get down to a mere trickle."

An hour before daybreak they stopped the wagon, poured water in a hat, and let each of the horses drink. "We'd best take time to eat," Rodelo said. "It'll be some time before we get the chance again."

"You sure they'll find us?"

"The Yaquis? You can bet on it."

They built a small fire and made coffee and fried bacon and eggs, eating with it some of the bread they had picked up at Sam's.

Rodelo was wary. Neither Harbin nor Badger was to be trusted; as for Gopher, it was unlikely he would start anything without some nudging from one of the others; but it paid to be careful. He avoided looking into the fire so his eyes would not be affected for night vision, and he made a point of hanging back from the others, keeping all of them always within sight.

Finally they put out the fire and moved on, the trail now taking them farther from the mountains and out into the bottom of the valley. Before them and around them was the Lechuguilla Desert.

Rodelo had no doubt as to what was happening on the other side of the mountains. The Yaquis, led by Hat, the shrewd old tracker who had taken the lead in the trailing of escaped convicts, would be searching for their trail. At first Hat would have swung south to cut the trails into the desert, then east and north. Finding no tracks, they might check beyond the river, but he doubted it because of the wagon. Not finding the wagon, the Indians would believe the outlaws still used it.

Hat would immediately grasp what had happened, and would cut for sign around the edges of the dunes. It might take a bit longer, but there would be a dozen or more Yaquis to make the search for tracks. By now Hat would have found their sign and be on the trail.

How much time did that leave? Hat would trail the horses to Gold City. Sam Burrows would tell them nothing, but it would not have taken long for Hat to decide they were again in a wagon—a wagon that must be abandoned within the next few hours. The team drawing the wagon could be released to save water and they would find their way back to Gold City. From that time on it would be a race to the south. They had saved a few hours, and every minute was important.

Joe Harbin stood in his stirrups and looked back the way they had come. There was no dust showing against the sky.

Badger was not looking back. They would know soon enough when the Yaquis started to close in. "We'd better spell the horses," he said, and all of them got down from the wagon and walked on.

Ahead of them were the famous Tinajas Altas, the "High Tanks" famous for saving many lives on the Devil's

Road, a road where many had also died. And to the south the country became rough.

Dan Rodelo dropped back beside Badger. "We're going to take another chance," he said. "I'm trying to lose those Yaquis."

Badger gave him an amused look. "You haven't a chance."

"We can play for time." He pointed to a long finger of rock that pushed into the desert not far ahead of them. "See that? Right beyond it there's a narrow pass through the mountains and we're going to take it, and hope they'll miss the turn-off and ride on south."

Badger looked doubtfully at the mountains. "There's a pass through *there*? I never heard of it."

"We'll leave the wagon," Rodelo said. "From here on we'll ride."

"I'll feel safer," Badger acknowledged.

The sun was well up in the sky when Rodelo guided the wagon into the lee of a sand dune, pulling in as close to the side of the dune as possible. Then, with Harbin and Gopher to help, he went up on the ridge of the dune and caved sand over on the wagon. In a few minutes it was covered; then, picking up handfuls of sand, they let it dribble out, sifting over what few tracks were visible.

After they had mounted up, Rodelo led them in an abrupt turn into the mountains, and in no more than fifteen minutes they were in a rapidly narrowing canyon that led them up a thousand feet in altitude in less than a mile. They crossed the Gilas on a narrow trail that showed no signs of recent use other than the tracks of bighorn sheep, a trail that wove in and around among peaks and ridges that lifted several hundred feet higher.

The route over the Gilas was not more than five or

six miles. They had watered the horses well before abandoning the wagon, emptying many of the cans and sacks and leaving them with the wagon. This lightened their load considerably, but Dan Rodelo knew what lay ahead perhaps better than any of them, and he knew it was not going to be easy.

"Are we going to make it?" Gopher asked him once.

"Some of us will," Rodelo replied.

He led them south, taking up the old Journey of Death, the Devil's Road. This led straight away south now for the Tinajas Altas, which were on a ridge that trailed off the end of the Gilas.

The day was hot. He slowed the pace of the horses, paused frequently for rest, and kept an eye on the trail behind. He noticed that Nora was taking the hard going surprisingly well.

She wore a skirt split for riding and a Mexican blouse, and like the others, she carried a gun. Joe Harbin seemed to have marked her for his own, but nothing was said, and she accepted the situation without comment, agreeing to nothing, rejecting no one. She was a shrewd girl, Rodelo decided, and one to watch.

It was Gopher who kept looking again and again to the rear. Harbin looked back rarely. He rode with the confidence of a man who has been through the mill, a hard-shouldered man, sure he needed no one.

The sun was now high overhead, the heat intense. In the brassy sky there was no cloud, only the sun whose rays seemed to blend into one great searing blast. The floor of the desert was hot beyond belief, and their horses plodded wearily, hopelessly, into the dead stillness. Far off to the south a dust devil sprang up, racing wildly across the flat desert floor.

Now Gopher no longer looked back. He sat his saddle, head hanging, simply enduring the heat.

"We had better hunt some shade," Rodelo commented, "or we'll kill our horses."

"Shade?" Harbin swore. "Where would you find shade?"

"Up in one of the canyons."

"Not me," Harbin said. "I'm headed for Mexico, and then the Gulf."

"You won't make it unless you give the horses a rest," Rodelo replied. "We've pushed them hard."

Harbin's face was streaked with sweat trails through the dust. His eyes were cruel when he turned to look at Rodelo. "I don't figure you," he said, "and I don't trust you. Just where do you come into this, anyway?"

"I'm in," Dan replied shortly. "I'm in up to my neck."

"We can change that," Harbin said, drawing up. He swung his horse a trifle to face Rodelo. "We can change that right here."

"Don't talk foolish," Rodelo replied. "You wouldn't have a chance without me. There's damn little water in this desert, and you've got to know where it is to find it."

"She knows." Harbin jerked his head to indicate Nora. "She told us about a place."

"A fat lot of good that will do you until you get there . . . and maybe that was a rain pool. It might all be gone by now. How long do you think an exposed pool will last in this heat?"

Tom Badger had been sitting his horse watching, withholding comment. He had nothing to lose if Harbin died; but, because of the water, a great deal to lose if Rodelo was telling the truth.

"Hold off, Joe," he said at last. "Dan's right. This

here country is hotter'n the floors of hell, and dryer. How long d'you think we'd last without water?"

Joe Harbin touched his parched lips, the cold hand of truth warning him as nothing else might have done. And there was no turning back now. It was go through or die.

"Aw, forget it!" he said. "Let's get on."

The trail showed plainly enough and Dan Rodelo watched him start off, followed by Gopher and Badger. Nora fell in beside him.

"He'll kill you, Dan," she said.

"Maybe."

"He's killed quite a few men."

"And someday he'll get killed—maybe by me."

She studied him. "Have you ever used a gun—like that, Dan?"

"Some," he admitted.

No use telling her how much, nor where and why. He knew far too little about Nora Paxton, and little enough about the others. As long as Joe Harbin felt he could kill him whenever he wanted to, Rodelo was sure of a fair chance. At this stage of the game, if Harbin guessed it might be a contest he would shoot him out of hand.

Rodelo mopped the sweat from his face and turned to look back. He could see nothing but dancing heat waves, shimmering their watery veil across the distance. If the Yaquis were back there, they were beyond those heat waves. . . . He rode on.

Only he himself knew what a chancy game he was playing, only he could know how much was at stake, and how wild the gamble he was taking. Yet what he was doing had to be done, for himself, at least. For in the last analysis a man must be true to himself first, and what was at stake in this was his own estimate of himself, and much, much more.

He rode with men he knew would kill, men who he knew had only hate for him, the interloper. Hate, and a question. Badger and Harbin, and maybe Gopher . . . any of them would kill him if the time was right. They would kill him for a canteen, a horse, a gun, or just because they hated him.

At the moment Harbin wanted to kill him because he talked too much to Nora, but Rodelo knew that within hours that would no longer be important. In the last hours it would be his own life that each man thought of and fought for. Beauty faded under the hot sun, and even sex came to nothing when one was faced with the raw and bloody face of death.

They all knew something of the country ahead, some by experience and some by hearsay. But only Dan Rodelo knew it well, and even he did not know it perfectly. No one did. No one wanted to remain there long enough to know it. There was no worse country anywhere than what lay before them. They did not have water enough. There were very few water holes, and those might not have water for more than one man, or one man and his horse.

Rodelo thought of the men riding ahead of him. Tom Badger was calm, cool, dangerous. Joe Harbin was a man of sudden, terrible passions, of long, brooding hatreds leading to sudden moments of killing fury. Gopher was not so much like a gopher as like a rat, quick to run, quick to squeal with fear, but if he was cornered he would be ready to slash out at anything, even himself.

And what of Nora? Rodelo was mystified by Nora.

Who was she? How had she come to be with these men? What did she want? Where was she going?

He had watched her. There were little refinements about her that puzzled him. She was, despite what one might have imagined, a girl with the instincts and perhaps the training of a lady. Her language was good. She had none of the careless, often rough talk of drifting frontier women. She was obviously not Joe Harbin's woman, although he had plans in that direction. Tom Badger resented her, and that was because she represented a threat to their escape.

Badger knew they dared carry no excess baggage. He knew their escape was going to be touch and go, and there shouldn't be anyone extra to worry about. Above all, Nora was another mouth that drank water.

They rode on through the blazing afternoon, heads hanging, mouths dry. Several times they drank a little water, and from time to time they stopped to sponge the mouths of their horses.

The mirages vanished, and the mountains far off to the south turned blue, then purple. The sun declined, the shadows grew long, and canyons bulged with darkness, ominous and threatening. The sky was streaked with flame; a few scattered clouds were edged with gold.

Dan Rodelo turned in his saddle and looked back. There was nothing. No sign of dust, only the quiet beauty of a desert when the sun has gone.

Tom Badger had slowed his pace. His face was streaked with dust and sweat. "How far to Tinajas Altas?" he asked.

"Too far." Rodelo gestured toward the low mountains along which they rode. "We'll cross over here and take a chance. There's a tank over there by Raven's Butte. Sometimes it has a little water."

He led the way. The going was no better and no worse than they had had before—a dim, rocky trail to be followed single file. They found the tank in a canyon southwest of Raven's Butte.

Rodelo swung down. "There's not enough here for the horses," he said, "but it will help."

He led each horse to drink, counted slowly while they drank to allow each horse an equal amount. When the horses had finished, the tank held no more than a cup of water.

When they left Raven's Butte, going south, they walked the horses. It was about seven miles, Dan Rodelo decided, to Tinajas Altas. There would be water there, and they could fill their canteens, then water the horses again. They would need every drop they could get.

"No Injuns," Gopher said triumphantly. "We lost 'em."

Harbin glanced at him contemptuously, but made no comment. It was Badger who spoke. "Don't you fool yourself, kid. They're back there, and they're comin' on."

"Do you really think they'll catch up with us?" Nora asked Rodelo.

"They're in no hurry," he said. "They can catch up all right, but they will wait until the desert has had time to work on us."

It was full dark by the time they reached Tinajas Altas, where they camped on the flat desert in a cove in the ridge. They built a small fire and made coffee. Nora sliced some of the bacon from a slab they had bought, among other food supplies, from Sam Burrows. They were not hungry, only exhausted from the heat and the savage travel over the blistering desert.

Presently the moon rose, and Tom Badger took up several canteens. "Let's see if there's water," he said.

Rodelo went ahead. He had been here only once before, but he found his way to the place where some traveler had left a rope trailing to help climbers. "The lowest tank is usually half full of sand, but there's water under it," he explained to Badger. "We'll try the upper tanks."

The water lay in basins of solid rock, hollowed by centuries of tumbling water in a stream channel, which was actually more of a waterfall. "There are dead bees in it sometimes," Rodelo explained, "but they're no problem."

Badger dipped up some of the water in his palm. It was cold and fresh. "Can't knock that. Anyway, I heard there were some rains down this away a few weeks back."

They filled the canteens, and then sat down on the rock beside the pool, refreshed by the coolness and drinking again and again.

"I just can't figure you," Badger said after a minute or two. "You don't size up like the law, but you sure ain't on the dodge. You done your time."

"Put me down as a man who likes money," Rodelo replied carelessly. "And where else could I get a piece of fifty thousand dollars? For that matter," he added ironically, "where could you?"

Badger chuckled. "You got me there, *amigo*. A piece of fifty thousand. . . . What we're all wonderin' about is how big a piece?"

"A three-way split, what else?"

"You think Joe will settle for that? After all, he was the one who pulled off the holdup."

Dan Rodelo got to his feet. "We'd best get back to the

horses. We'd be in fine shape now if Joe was to take a notion to ride out and leave us, wouldn't we?"

They climbed down the way they had come, going hand over hand, their feet against the steeply slanting rock wall. On the ground below, Rodelo added, speaking softly, "Tom, you know as well as I do, the size of that split is going to be decided by the Yaquis, not us."

"Yeah," Badger said gloomily. "They could trim us down a mite."

The night was cold, and they took turn and turn about standing watch. In the last hour before dawn, Joe Harbin shook them awake. Over a small, quick fire of dried-out creosote wood, they made coffee and finished the bacon. Before the desert was more than gray, they were in the saddle once more, horses well watered, the desert stretching wide toward the border, now only a short distance away.

The rocky ridge of the mountains was their guide line; the desert floor was broken here and there by black, ugly outcroppings of ancient lava. There was creosote brush, occasional agave, and cholla.

The sun was not yet above the horizon when Joe Harbin rode up from the rear. "We got comp'ny," he said.

They drew up and turned to look. Far off they saw a thin column of smoke pointing a beckoning finger at the sky.

"Well, we expected it," Badger said. "They must've tried several routes. The smoke will call 'em in." He glanced back again. "No use waitin' for 'em."

They went on. The sun rose, the day's heat began, and they deliberately slowed their pace. Gopher wanted to get on, to run. "It would kill your horse, kid," Badger said mildly. "You'll need that horse."

They saw no Indians. Rodelo looked only occasionally to the rear. He watched ahead and on both sides, for Indians could come from anywhere, and there might well be Yaquis somewhere ahead, returning from the Gulf, for instance.

"You're bearing east," Harbin said suddenly. "What's the idea?"

"Pinacate," Rodelo replied. "Some of the roughest country this side of hell, but some tanks of water, too . . . and some places to fort up if need be."

"Won't that give us further to go?"

"Very little. The Gulf is south of us now. Adair Bay is due south."

Nobody talked then for a time. Later they saw another smoke, off to the west. The horses slowed to a walk, and when Rodelo swung down and led his horse, the others did likewise. Again, Nora fell in beside him.

She was showing her weariness now. Her face was drawn, her eyes hollow. "I had no idea it would be like this," she said.

"Whenever you can," Rodelo advised her, "drink. Dehydration begins to dull your senses before you realize. Some say you shouldn't drink at all the first twenty-four hours in the desert, but that's insanity. Others say to make your water last. But it's better to drink plenty when you're close to water, and keep drinking. You'll stand a better chance of getting through."

"Will we make it, Dan?" It was the first time she had called him by his name.

He shrugged. "We'll make it . . . some of us will. But we've got pure hell ahead of us, and don't you doubt it."

He gestured to the east. "This is the Camino del Diablo . . . the Devil's Road we've been talking about.

Between three and four hundred people died along it during the Gold Rush."

Here the desert was sprinkled with creosote bush, clumps of cholla, and an occasional sahuaro or ocotillo. They found their way through it, usually riding single file, maintaining a generally southerly route.

When they came to a small rise Joe Harbin halted. "Why don't we just lay up and ambush 'em?" he asked. "We could be rid of them once and for all."

"And have them ride around us?" Dan answered. "They could cut us off from water."

"What water?" Tom Badger had turned his head and was watching Rodelo.

"There's Tule Wells, but it's a mite far east, I'd say. We can save time by striking right for Papago Tanks."

And now the desert began to be broken and rugged. Volcanic cones stood up in half a dozen places; and Rodelo, swinging wide, indicated a deep crater to the others.

This was the edge of the Pinacate country. To the south it grew worse, with miles of pressure-ridge lava, sand dunes, and broken country almost devoid of water. Through all that country there was only a trail or two, so far as he knew. Miles and miles of it were broken rock, razor-edged lava that could cripple a horse or a man on foot within hours. There was no life out there except occasional bighorns, coyotes, and rattlers. But they must weave a way through, then make a run for it across the sand to the bay.

They made dry camp among the black rocks, forting up for a fight that did not come. At daybreak they moved out again, drinking often from their canteens, seeing their water supply dwindle, bit by bit.

Tempers grew short. Joe Harbin cursed his horse, and Gopher muttered under his breath and glowered at everybody. Dan fought to keep his temper. Nora alone seemed assured, calm. Her face was haggard, her eyes hollow, and at night when she dismounted she almost fell from her horse, but she did not complain.

That night the Yaquis closed in, but not to fight.

They came swiftly, suddenly, as Harbin was selecting a camp, another dry camp.

From out of a seemingly empty desert the Indians came in a swift short charge, a flurry of shots, and then disappeared down a draw toward the desert ahead.

Flattened out among the rocks, they waited, guns ready, but the Yaquis did not return. After a while, Badger got to his feet, expecting a shot.

All was still. Twilight shadows were deep, the desert held no sound. Badger walked to the horses as the others slowly got up.

He spoke suddenly, his voice oddly strained, high-pitched for him. "Look," he said.

A bullet had struck their largest canteen, and the water had drained out on the sand. Only a dark spot remained where it had soaked away.

"We'll make coffee," Rodelo said, "there's enough left for that."

CHAPTER 6

DAN RODELO LOOKED at the stars, felt the coolness of the desert night, and was thankful. There was not much in the life that lay behind him that had been pleasant or easy. Only there was a memory of his mother long ago, and of a home where all was comfort. How long had that been?

Now he rode a desert trail with men of violence, and he himself had been a man of violence, living where the weight of a fist and the speed of a gun were all that spelled the difference between life and death. And now he fought out this last, desperate fight among desperate men.

Desperate men . . . and a girl.

What kind of person was she? Why did she want to make this trip into the desert with such men as these? Dan Rodelo had thought out every step of what he had to do. The one thing he had not counted on was Nora Paxton.

Four men and a woman, ringed with death, a death that might come from the Yaquis in pursuit, but could just as likely come from the desert itself.

Their biggest canteen was holed, the others almost empty. The horses would need most of what there was, and at best, there would be a swallow for each of them. When they rode out at daybreak there would be no water left.

Without water, how long could a man live and travel under that sun, in that parching heat? A day, perhaps . . . or two days. He knew of one man who had lived three days beyond the point where he should have died, lived by sheer guts, by hatred, by the driving will to live and get revenge.

There was water enough for coffee, and when the coffee was made they sat together and drank it, each busy with his own thoughts. Dan Rodelo knew what might be done in these circumstances, but he was no murderer, and he could come to only one conclusion, the same one he had arrived at in the beginning: to see the thing through to the end . . . and at the end he must tell them the truth.

It would mean a shooting, of course, and he was not the gunman that Joe Harbin was. Possibly he was faster than Tom Badger, but even of that he could not be sure. He had been a fool to try what he was trying, but that was the sort of man he was—not very wise, not very shrewd, using only what he had, which was a certain toughness, a stamina, a stubborn unwillingness to quit.

"What about it?" Joe looked up at Rodelo. "You are the man who is supposed to know where there's water."

"We'll try. We'll move out by daybreak."

"If they let us," Badger said.

"They will," Rodelo said.

He was somehow sure of that, sure of it because he had known Indians before. There was something in the Indian that made him torture, not only to bring suffering to an enemy, but to test how much he could stand. To the Indian bravery was all, bravery and stamina, so it was like him to test his enemies, to know how great his victory had been.

And Hat was no fool. Time was on his side, and he

could afford to hang back, to let the heat and thirst and the fierce tempers of the men they followed do their work.

The shooting they had done was only a preliminary test, a plumb line into the well of their resistance. The pursued men had reacted suddenly, sharply, so the Yaquis knew the time was not yet, and they would follow for another day, perhaps two days.

"Do you know where there's water?" Nora asked.

"I know where it might be. Don't expect a spring. If there are springs in this country I never met anybody who knew of them. There are tanks like those at Tinajas Altas or at Raven's Butte . . . there's Papago Tanks, Tule Wells, and some isolated places. I think I can find them."

"You'd better," Harbin said.

Rodelo glanced at him. "Don't push your luck," he said quietly, "because I have at least one advantage."

"You?" Harbin sneered.

"I know just how good you are with a gun, but you don't know anything about me."

"There's nothing I need to know."

He spoke abruptly, almost carelessly, but Dan Rodelo was sure the remark had hit home. Harbin was naturally suspicious, trusting no one, and he would be doubly suspicious now. He would ask himself just what Rodelo meant. Was he, perhaps, a known gunfighter using a different name? If so, who would he be?

Harbin ran through them in his mind, trying to place the whereabouts of each one. Jim Courtright, Ben Thompson, Commodore Perry Owens, Doc Holliday, John Bull, Farmer Peel . . . one by one he named them off to himself. But there must be some he didn't know.

Rodelo had hoped for just one thing, to make Harbin curious, and wary of him.

These were not desert men, Dan Rodelo knew that much. Both Badger and Harbin were men of the plains. Tom Badger was part Indian; he had been a buffalo hunter and then a cow thief. He had more than once been involved in the holdup robberies of stages, and had ridden in a cattle war.

Harbin had been a cowhand, a fireman on the Denver and Rio Grande, a hired gunman in several township and cattle wars, and finally a holdup man. His first killings had been over card games.

Whatever they knew of wilderness was what they knew of the Plains states and the mountain country on the east slope of the Rockies. Neither was likely to know the little tricks of desert survival . . . though possibly Badger might.

AT DAYBREAK THEY moved out, mouths dry, lips cracked and stiff, every movement of their eyes painful under inflamed lids. In the distance, but not very far off, there was a low dust cloud that kept pace with them. Harbin glowered at it, and swore.

They could no longer travel with any speed. The Pinacate country was all about them, broken lava, deep craters, pinnacles of rock, and everywhere was a thick growth of cholla. Some desert dwellers called one kind of cholla the "jumping cactus," for when a hand came near it or when you passed too close the cactus seemed to leap out and deliberately impale you upon its needle-sharp thorns.

The cholla is covered with knobs about the thickness

of a short banana, and these knobs are covered with spines, each one capable of causing a painful sore. The joints of the cholla break off easily, for this is the way the plant is propagated. The cholla grows in thick clumps, spreading in some cases out to cover acres, and it seems to love best the crevices in the lava. In some places clumps of cholla may climb halfway up a small volcanic cone, and their lemon yellow spines glow on the dark desert like distant lights.

To ride among them made every step a risk. The joints broke off and stuck in the horses' legs, in the riders' clothing, even in the saddle ladder. Nothing was safe from the thorns. Once in the flesh, they seemed hooked there, and were both difficult and painful to remove.

Dan Rodelo rode in the lead, weaving a precarious way among the outcroppings of jagged lava and the cholla. It was ugly country. At times they had to cross short stretches of lava where a slip would be almost sure to mean a broken leg for a horse. Once they skirted a crater that must have been at least four hundred feet deep. In the bottom were several scattered sahuaro, and some of the big cactus had grown at a point where the ridge was broken like a breach in a wall. Clusters of cholla were all about them, and clumps of cat-claw. Far off he could see a bighorn watching from a volcanic cone. This was the heart of the Pinacate country.

Nora closed in beside him. He was shocked at her face. Her lips had cracked, and they had bled. "Is it much further, Dan?" she asked. "I mean to the bay?"

"A good bit."

"What's going to happen?"

He looked at her, and he was worried by the same thought. "Too much, I'm afraid. You keep your head down, d'you hear, when the Yaquis come. And after that . . . well, you know how Joe Harbin feels."

"What're you two talkin' about?" Harbin shouted. "That's my woman you're a-talkin' to, Rodelo, and don't you forget it."

Dan turned a bit in the saddle. "She will decide that, I think."

"Like hell she will! I've decided it. She's mine, and any time you want to argue the question you speak up."

Dan sat easy on his saddle, but the thong was off his six-shooter. "Don't ride that reputation too hard, Joe. Somebody might want to try it out."

"Any time."

Talking hurt his lips, and Dan Rodelo did not reply. He squinted his eyes against the sun, searching the lava for familiar signs, but he saw none. Yet the tank had to be near.

All morning they had ridden without water. Now the sun was high, the horses moved with lagging steps. Suddenly he saw a white blaze on a dark rock up ahead. At the same time a bee shot by him, flying a straight course.

The horses smelled the water and quickened their pace. And then they all saw it. Nora stared, and then turned her face away. Tom swore bitterly. In the tank, which was half filled with water, lay a dead bighorn, and it had been dead several days.

Joe Harbin turned on Rodelo. "This the kind of water you take us to?"

"It ain't his fault. Be reasonable," Tom said quietly. "We're in trouble, but we ain't goin' to get out of it by fightin' amongst ourselves."

Gopher looked at Rodelo, his eyes haunted by fear.

"We've got another chance," Rodelo said, "about an hour from here."

Wearily, they climbed into their saddles once more and started the reluctant horses toward the southeast. Fear rode with them, for now their margin of safety was gone. All were feeling the effects of dehydration, which had been growing with each passing hour. Rodelo, who had saturated himself with water when he had the chance, was in better shape than the others. Nora had followed his advice to some degree.

Dan Rodelo studied the terrain as they moved along. Once down on the flat, there would be no water. He knew that Papago Tanks, usually holding some water, often quite a lot, were somewhere near. But there were few landmarks. The terrain, weird as it was, had a sameness that made locating any spot difficult.

He could feel the effort his horse was making, could feel the heaviness in its muscles, the desire to stop, no matter what. When they had put a mile behind them, he drew up. "We'd best walk," he said, "if we want our horses to last."

Though loath to do so, they dismounted, and Rodelo started to walk on.

Nobody felt like eating, nor was it wise to eat, with no water. Rodelo's lips were painfully cracked, but they scarcely bled, for with dehydration any scratch dried up almost at once. He walked slowly, setting a pace easier for those behind him to follow. A careless touch on a bit of rock in passing was like touching red-hot iron from a forge.

Ahead of them he saw a black ridge, shading off in places to a dull red, depending on the way the sunlight fell. Was that the place?

Squinting his eyes, he looked for some familiar landmark. He knew that in the wilderness any place may have many different aspects, which is the reason why seasoned travelers watch their back trail, to know how the country will look on their return journey. A slightly different view of terrain, under different conditions of light, can often make a surprising difference in appearance.

Rodelo's brain was sluggish. He struggled with his thoughts, trying to remember what he knew of this place . . . if it *was* the place. Finally, he started on once more, tugging to get his horse moving again.

The rocks were corrugated and rough, each edge like a serrated knife, tearing at their boots or clothing. Turning to look back, he was shocked at the looks of those who followed him. Nora's blouse had been torn by cactus, her boots were badly scuffed; her buckskin divided skirt was standing up best of all, but even that was showing signs of the rough travel.

Gopher's thin face looked strained, his lips ugly with cracks and bleeding. Badger and Harbin were caricatures of their original selves. The small procession was scattered over several hundred yards, and had the Yaquis attacked at that moment they would have had an easy victory.

At the next step Rodelo saw the track of a bighorn. There were a lot of the desert bighorns in the Pinacate country, and as his eyes searched the ground he saw another, somewhat smaller track, partly overlaid by the track of a desert fox. All pointed the same direction. He stopped and studied the slopes carefully, then turned in among the rocks.

He had not found the trail by which he had once come

to Papago Tanks, but he was trying to find his way by deduction, with an assist from the tracks he had seen. Much of the rock here was polished by wind and blown sand, and it was slippery underfoot. This was a wild land, gloomy and forbidding, a place normally to be avoided, but it was here he hoped to find water.

Suddenly he saw the bluish basaltic rock he remembered. He veered a little, went down between two great slabs of volcanic rock, and was on the tiny sandy beach by the water hole. At the base of a twenty-foot drop a hollow had been worn by falling water and churning rock fragments to a depth of four or five feet. Back of it, and close by, was another pool, at least a dozen feet in diameter. There the water was shaded by a slight leaning of the rock, and the water below was cold and clear.

"Let the horses drink from the near pool," Rodelo said. "We'll drink from the one further back."

He stooped and scooped a mouthful of the water, sucking it from his palm and feeling the coolness of it bring life to the parched tissues of his mouth. He let a few drops trickle down his throat, and felt his stomach contract. He drank slowly, taking only a swallow at a time. Then he took the canteen from his horse and filled it, and after that he filled Nora's.

Then he led the horses to water, allowed them a little and took them away, and after a bit came back with them for more.

This was not the end of their troubles, he knew. They could no longer use their largest canteen and they could not carry enough water. How far was it to Adair Bay? Twenty miles perhaps? Twenty-five?

With the horses in such bad shape they could not hope to make it in a day. After some rest here, they might make it in two days. So far they had been lucky; and he, better than any of the others, knew how lucky.

He glanced at the sky. It would be hot tomorrow; and he knew that when the temperature is 110 degrees at breathing level it may be fifty degrees hotter on the sand underfoot. In this arroyo where they now were it could be bitterly cold at night, but during the day heat was sucked up from the sands, and the stifling hot, drying winds drained the moisture from the tissues and left man or animal dried out like old shoe leather that has been exposed to the sun. In such heat, even twenty-four hours without water could kill a man.

Nora came up beside him. "What are we going to do now?" she asked.

"We'll rest, eat, drink some more, and get ready to start for the coast."

"Do you think there will be trouble?"

He considered that. "Yes, I am afraid so. The Indians are out there. They've got to take us now, and they know it."

"What can we do?"

"Drink . . . drink all you can hold. Saturate all your tissues with it. You'll last longer if you do."

He led the horses to water once more, then picketed them near some mesquite brush and clumps of burrow bush.

He was gathering a few sticks of dried-out wood when Joe Harbin came up to him. Gopher was with him, Tom Badger bringing up the rear.

"That's good water, Rodelo," Harbin said. "I'll apologize. You knew where you were goin', all right."

"I still do."

"What's that mean?"

"We're not out of the woods yet, Harbin. It's maybe twenty-five miles or so down to the coast. That's two days, at best."

"Hell, I've ridden seventy miles a day more'n once."

"On horses like these? They're in bad shape, Harbin."

"They'll make it."

"Take your time, Joe," Badger suggested. "Maybe he's right."

"Like hell he is! He's stallin' for time. We just don't need him any more."

Dan Rodelo got up from the pile of sticks he was preparing. "We'll make some coffee," he said to Nora, "and have something to eat. The hardest time is still ahead of us."

He looked around at Harbin. "You need me, all right. You need me now worse than ever. You've still got a fight with those Indians . . . and don't underestimate them. They've been trackin' down escaped convicts for years, and they get most of them."

"Let 'em come—the sooner the better."

"That's dune sand west of here, Harbin. There's places out there where a horse can sink belly-deep, and every time he tries to get out he sinks deeper. And the same for men. Or suppose your canteen gets holed? You're a long way from being out of the woods yet. You got any idea how many cons got this far? I can name you a dozen . . . but they lost out between here and the coast."

"I don't believe it."

"He makes sense," Badger said. "We'd better look to our hole card."

Gopher brought more sticks and added to the fire.

Nora looked at him and asked, "Why do they call you Gopher?"

He grinned at her. "I was forever tryin' to dig out. Made so many tunnels they called me Gopher. It was partly because of him"—he indicated Tom Badger. "He was the Badger, and bigger than me, so they called me the Gopher."

They ate and drank, and finally one by one they lay down exhausted on the sand.

"You cover up," Rodelo warned Nora. "The wind will start coming down this arroyo, and it will be cold."

"Cold?" She was incredulous.

"You'll be chilled to the bone, take it from me. You cover up."

He looked in the direction of the coast. From a high point a man might see it all, laid out there before him, but it would be deceiving. Desert country has a way of concealing its obstacles: canyons that don't seem to be there until one stands on the very edge of them, and lava flows that would ruin a new pair of boots in a few miles.

Somehow he knew. Tomorrow would be the day . . . tomorrow.

CHAPTER 7

DAN RODELO SLIPPED the thong off his six-shooter and worked his fingers. He wanted no trouble. He had come here for a purpose, and if he could accomplish that purpose without a gunfight he would be satisfied. How he would fare in a gun battle with Joe Harbin he had no idea, but he knew that Harbin had not killed men by accident. He was a good shot and a tough man.

Tom Badger was shrewd and careful, willing to let the others fight. And neither of them planned to let Gopher come in for anything.

Rodelo had gone to prison for a crime he had not committed. That rankled, but what hurt most was that others believed him guilty. Above all else, he meant to prove himself innocent, and then he would drift out of the country. He no longer wanted any part of those who had distrusted him, who had lost faith in him so quickly.

Nora was at the fire, and the coffee water was boiling. Badger hunkered down, back a bit from the flames, and faced partly away from them. "So far so good, Danny," he said. "You brought us to water."

"Better tank up," Rodelo answered. "Drink all you can. We've got the worst of all waiting for us out there."

Harbin snorted. "I can do the rest of it standin' on my head."

Rodelo shrugged. "You pick your own way of doing

it, Harbin, but I'll see no man die out there if I can help it. There's a belt of shifting dunes between here and the coast, miles of them, and not a drop of water to be had."

Harbin looked at him. "You sure like to make a big man of yourself, don't you?"

Rodelo made no reply. Harbin's frustration and irritation, coupled with the harsh travel, had brought him to a murderous mood, and Rodelo realized it.

"Coffee's ready," Nora said. "Come and get it while it's hot."

"I'll have some," Rodelo said. "A cup of coffee would taste right good."

Nora filled a cup and handed it to him, but Harbin reached over so suddenly he almost spilled the coffee in grabbing for the cup. "I'll take that!" he said sharply.

"Sure," Rodelo replied mildly, "you have it, Harbin."

Harbin stared at him angrily. "What's the matter? You yella? You afraid to fight?"

Rodelo shrugged. He was half smiling. "What's there to fight about? We'll all get coffee. You can have the first cup."

"Maybe I'll have the second too!" Harbin was prodding him; but the time was not right, and Rodelo could wait.

"All right, you have the second too."

"And maybe I'll take it all!"

"What about us, Joe?" Badger spoke quietly. "I'd like a cup myself."

Nora held out a cup to Dan. "Take this. There's no sense in bickering over a cup of coffee."

Instantly, Joe Harbin slapped the cup from her hand and grabbed for his gun. He drew and fired so quickly that his shot missed, smashing into the just filled waterbags behind Rodelo.

Rodelo, close to him, went in on a long dive, his powerful right shoulder catching Harbin on the hip and knocking him spinning to the ground. Before he could get a good grip on his gun again, Rodelo kicked it from his hand.

With a grunted oath, Harbin came off the sand in a lunge, but he pulled his punch too wide and Dan Rodelo caught him on the cheekbone with a wicked right as he came in. Harbin, stopped in his tracks, was perfectly set up for the sweeping left, and he went down hard.

Instantly, Badger leaped in and grabbed Rodelo. "Easy now! Let's not be fightin'!"

Stunned, Harbin lay still for a moment. When he got up he was quiet. "All right, Rodelo," he said. "I'll kill you for that."

His voice was cold and even. The man who spoke was not the man Rodelo had knocked down, scarcely the man he had known for all those months in prison. For the first time Dan Rodelo felt something like fear. Yet he stood quietly and looked at Harbin.

"You'll be a fool if you try, Harbin," he said. "You're out of prison. You're in Mexico. In a matter of a day or two you'll be aboard Isacher's boat and headed for Mazatlan. But believe me, you'll need me from here until you get to the Gulf. You'll need me until you get your feet on that boat."

There was a growing welt on Harbin's cheekbone, a thin cut on his jaw. Harbin's fingers touched them gingerly. "You marked me," he said almost wonderingly. "Nobody ever put a mark on me before."

He took up his coffee and, making no effort to retrieve his gun, walked off and sat down on a rock. Nora filled cups for Badger, Gopher, and Rodelo, and finally for herself. Nobody talked. They drank their coffee, the wind down the arroyo grew chill. Dan added wood to the fire, going out into the darkness for branches or roots of dried mesquite and creosote.

The fire blazed up, the smoke smelled good, the stars became brighter and the wind colder.

"Is there water down by the Gulf?" Badger asked.

"Some . . . and some of it is bad."

"But you know the good springs?"

"Sure he does," Harbin spoke up. "You can bet he knows. He knows just about everything."

Badger strolled over to the waterbags. The sand was damp under them. He knew what he would see when he lifted the sacks, for he had seen the bullet strike. The bags had been piled together; now they were flat and empty. Each of them had been holed by the bullet, cutting a corner from one sack, going through another and into the third.

Harbin watched Badger examine the bags and drop them back on the ground. "We still got two canteens," he said. "That should last us."

"And the horses?"

"We'll water them before we leave. They'll make it."

The horses were in bad shape and they all knew it; they were in no condition for a grueling ride through the last of the lava, and then the tough travel over the deep sand of the dunes.

Harbin came over, picked up his gun, rubbed the sand from it, and slid it into his holster.

"Where are they?" Nora asked. "The Indians, I mean."

"Out there. They're where they can see our fire, maybe

even within the sound of our voices. They've seen all this before, you know. We'll have to keep a good lookout tonight."

He got up and walked over to the horses. Leading them to water, he allowed them to drink their fill. He noticed that the campfire showed scarcely at all when a man was well away from it. He let the horses take their time, then led them to some mesquite brush and picketed them nearer the fire.

Now for the first time he realized how tired he was, but he did not dare to sleep. He could trust no one of them, perhaps not even Nora. He had not figured her out at all, but then she could know nothing about him either.

He tried to remember all he knew about this country, and could recall only a little, most of it quite general. These natural tanks were the only water he knew of south of Tinajas Altas on which a man could rely, and even they might on occasion be empty or down to mere dregs. But there must have been rain not very long ago, for the tanks were well filled and the water was sweet. West of Pinacate was an area to be avoided. He had never penetrated far in that direction and it might be passable, but there were hundreds of small cones there, and rough lava flows—desperately bad country to cross. To the east it was nearly as bad, but a ghost of a trail went that way and just at the base of the two highest peaks there were some tanks. He had never seen them, but a Yuma Indian had told him of them. This Indian had learned of them from the Sand Papagos, who had once lived in the Pinacate country.

Whether there was water or not, it would be a safer route, although somewhat longer. There were other tanks at the southern tip of Pinacate, but none of them or those to the east were reliable.

Why not, he asked himself, bring it to a showdown now? Yet the moment he thought of it he knew he dared do nothing of the kind. In the first place, he was outnumbered; in the second, he hoped to bring it off without a shooting if he could manage it. In a way, he was waiting, just as the Indians were, for them to play out. At the same time he knew he was giving them every break he could . . . was it because of Nora? Or some forgotten remnant of humanitarian impulse within him?

He could slip away and hide out in the desert. After all, one of the remaining canteens was his own. But without him there was little chance they would survive. A chance, yes, but a very small one.

The wind was cold. Rodelo looked up at the stars. The desert or mountain man was forever lifting his eyes to the peaks or to the stars; it was no wonder that men of the wilderness knew so much about the flight of birds and the habits of animals. In cities a man's eyes were on the ground, or rarely above eye level.

He went back toward the fire, but stood back from it, beyond the edge of the light. He wanted to offer no target if one of the Indians decided now was the time.

"We've got to mount guard," Badger said.

Harbin got up. "I'll take first watch." He turned to Nora. "Come on, let's go."

"Why me?" Nora's surprise was obvious.

"You can keep me comp'ny. Else I'm likely to fall asleep."

Tom Badger chuckled, but made no comment. Joe turned on him. "What's so funny about that?"

"Nothin'. I was just wonderin' who was going to keep Gopher and me awake . . . and Danny."

"Maybe I should share the watch with each of you," Nora suggested with amusement.

"We could roll the dice to see who takes which watch. Low roll to take the first watch."

"That ain't necessary," Joe said.

"Let's have the dice, Dan," Badger said. "I think that's a fair idea."

He shook the dice and rolled them out on a flat rock. A five and a four.

Gopher rolled snake eyes, a two, and Rodelo followed with a six. Joe took the dice, threw them irritably . . . a pair of fives.

"That gives you the dawn watch, Joe," Badger said. He started to pick up the dice, but Nora reached over and took them from him. "You're forgetting me."

"You don't have to stand a watch," Harbin said.

"I agree with Joe," Rodelo said quietly. "You will need your rest, Nora."

"So will all of you. After all, I am in this too, I'm riding a horse, I'm drinking water, and I will do my share." She rolled the dice . . . a four.

"That gives me second watch, I think," she said.

Rodelo took up his blanket. "Whoever is on watch," he said, "keep an eye on the horses. If we lose them we've had it."

Gopher, first on watch, went to a rock near the horses, a position from which he could look over the camp without being approached from behind. Rodelo found a place in the lee of a rock that could shelter him from the cold wind blowing down the arroyo.

But there was more to it than that. Scattered on the

ground were the smaller twigs broken from the firewood they had gathered, and it was virtually impossible for anyone to approach without a stick cracking. Wrapped in his blanket, Rodelo took a last look at the fire, at the positions of the others, and then went to sleep.

CHAPTER 8

RODELO WAS AWAKENED by Nora's careful, almost noiseless movements when she went to relieve Gopher.

"It's only me, Gopher," she said. "It's my turn to take the watch."

"You don't have to, ma'am. I can stick it out."

"You get some sleep while you can. I think tomorrow will be a rough day."

"I'd like to do it, ma'am. It would be a real pleasure for a lady like yourself."

"No . . . you get some rest. And Gopher, drink a lot of water. That's what Dan has been advising me to do."

Gopher was standing up, and Rodelo could see him. He heard his voice, very low. "I like him, ma'am—that Rodelo, I mean. I think he's square. I guess . . . I guess I never met many who were really on the level. Not like him."

"He was in prison."

"But he wasn't guilty, ma'am!" Gopher said quickly. "Everybody knew that. He just got himself roped into the deal when Joe Harbin grabbed that gold. Folks thought he'd connived with Joe, but that ain't so, and many's the time in prison I heard Joe say as much. He figured it was a good joke on Rodelo."

Gopher was silent for a moment, then he added, "Joe

could have cleared Rodelo, but he didn't. You see, the way I heard it, after Joe stood up that payroll he made a clean getaway, then ran into Rodelo on the trail and they rode on together, the way folks do when they meet up like that. Only it seems Rodelo knew about that payroll and they figured him to be in on it."

"You'd better get some rest, Gopher," Nora said. "Tomorrow is another long hot day."

Dan Rodelo lay quiet. Well, Gopher had told her, and from Gopher she would believe it, for Gopher had nothing to gain by lying. Suddenly, he was glad she knew, even though she did not, yet, know all of it. Nobody knew it all but himself, not even the people back at the mine who had been willing enough to buy the idea that he was a thief.

He lay there, half awake, half asleep, for some time, and finally eased from under the blankets and belted on his gun again. He went at once to the tank and drank, deep and long. Out in the night a coyote sounded, and he listened, but heard no echo. The Indians said that was the way to tell . . . that a man imitating a coyote would also make an echo, but there was something in the timbre of a coyote's howl that did not echo. Rodelo had never decided whether this was true or not, but it seemed to be, the few times he had put it to the test.

He walked out to where Nora was on guard. She looked around quickly, her gun muzzle lifting. He grinned in the darkness. No nonsense about her—she was ready for trouble.

"It's me," he said quietly.

"My time isn't up yet."

"Do you object to some extra rest? I was awake, and I might as well be awake out here as back there."

He seated himself near her. The night was still. Out upon the desert nothing moved. The stars held still in the sky; the black bulk of Pinacate loomed off to the south.

"I didn't expect the desert to be like this," she said. "So much growing, and all."

"The plants have learned how to survive, each in its own way. Some of them store water against the long drouth, and some seeds will only grow when a certain amount of water has fallen. Most desert plants hold back their leaves or blossoms until the right amount of rain comes, then they blossom quickly and get it over with."

Rodelo listened for a moment, then he said, "Did you ever look over a desert from high up on a mountain? The greasewood looks as if it had been planted, it's so evenly spaced. Well, it's spaced like that because it needs to draw water from the area around it."

They sat quietly for a time, and then he spoke again. "I don't get it. What are you doing here? I mean, what have you got to gain?"

"What have I to lose?"

"Your life means nothing to you?"

"Of course it does." She looked around at him. "It might be that I want that gold, too. Or part of it."

"You'd be wasting your time. You'll never see a single coin of it."

"Joe Harbin may feel otherwise."

He was silent while again he assayed the darkness. "He won't," he said then. "Joe isn't the kind to let one bit of that gold slip through his fingers if he can help it. If you're counting on that, you better forget it."

"I can handle Joe."

"Maybe you can, at that." There was an edge of sarcasm in his tone. "Jake Andrews was no Sunday school teacher, either."

"What's that to you?"

"Nothing . . . nothing at all."

"Jake was all right. He was a good enough man in his way, but he listened to Clint. Jake heard about the gold, heard of it from Joe Harbin's woman, because one night when Joe was drunk he did some bragging. Clint kept after him until Jake agreed to go and have a look for that gold."

"What about you and Jake?"

She turned her eyes on him, but in the darkness he could not see their expression. "What about us?" she said.

"I mean . . . you don't seem his sort of girl."

"Any sort of girl was Jake's sort. He pulled me out of a wrecked train up in Wyoming. I was on fire—my clothes, I mean. He put the fire out, and helped me get away from the Indians who wrecked the train . . . if they were Indians."

"What do you mean?"

"I always thought Jake was in that himself. Only when he found me he pulled out, very fast. But he treated me all right. Jake was a hard man, and something of a brute, but he had a queer streak in him. He talked roughly to me, as he did to everyone, but he was oddly gentle too. He wanted to marry me."

"He was a rancher, wasn't he?"

"Indians drove off his herd and burned him out. He had some idea of going into Mexico and starting again."

"So now you're here." He started out over the desert, keeping his ears attuned to night sounds. Their voices were low, barely above a whisper. "Right in the middle of hell."

The wind was cold, and unconsciously they had drawn closer together. Dan looked toward the camp. All lay still, sleeping. At the fire only a few embers glowed among the ashes. His eyes searched the darkness for movement, for any shape that did not belong there.

He knew the Yaquis were close, knew they were skilled man-hunters, and he knew what the fifty dollars a head would mean to them. And there was the added attraction of the girl, of Nora. Of course, they would not bring her back. Nobody knew about her, and it was unlikely that questions would be asked.

As for himself, he wasn't wanted anywhere, but Hat wanted his boots, which would be reason enough. And, of course, they wanted to make a clean sweep.

"If you're the last one alive," he said, "and the Indians take you, you might talk them into taking you to Sam Burrows. He'd give them a hundred dollars for you. Tell them that—it might save your life."

"And otherwise?"

"There are some springs on Adair Bay, and there's to be a boat there to pick up a man named Isacher. He's dead, so don't worry about him. If not that boat, there are fishing boats along from time to time."

"And what if we all come through? Or if it is just you and Joe Harbin?"

He looked at her thoughtfully in the darkness. "Then I suppose you will have to choose, Joe Harbin or me."

He turned suddenly and took her by the shoulders, and for a moment he held her, looking into her face. Then he bent his head and kissed her, lightly, on the lips. "There . . . when the times comes, that may help."

AT NO GREAT distance, at a place where the basalt had faulted, Hat lay in a niche in the rock. It was a place where he was sheltered from the cold wind, and high enough above the sand so that he had a good view of the camp with its red, winking eye marking the fire. He could distinguish occasional movement near the horses, or about the camp.

They were standing watch, of course. He had expected that. In fact, he had expected about everything that had happened thus far. There was not much a running man could do when he got into the Pinacate country. The only difference was that someone here knew about the water holes.

He knew now who it was. It was simply a matter of reading the sign right, seeing who scouted in the right directions. It was the man with the new boots . . . Rodelo.

They were carrying something they could not have had when they left the prison, and it was too heavy to be supplies. He had seen the tracks of the pack horse that carried it, and he had seen where it rested at night.

Hat had his own plans, but they were not new. He had used them many times before, and they had been successful. He had never attacked until they reached the dunes or the beach.

Here, among the broken lava flows around Pinacate,

there were too many sheltered places. They could defend themselves too well, and usually they were still in shape to put up a stiff fight. He could wait until the dunes and drift sand broke their spirit. None of them carried much water, and that was his first target.

His plan was simplicity itself. Get them out in the dunes. They would have had little to eat or drink, and if their horses had lived this far they had reached their limit. There was shelter in the dunes for him and for his warriors, and they could move easily. The escaped prisoners would be trying for the coast, and he would edge them back from it, make them struggle among the dunes until the last of their water and the last of their strength was exhausted. After that, it would be easy enough.

Usually they died among the dunes, but occasionally one or two would reach the shore. Then he would push them toward one of the two or three poisoned springs nearby, keeping them away from those where fresh if slightly brackish water might be found. Several of the escaped prisoners in the past had been dead before he shot them . . . the bullet hole was evidence of his capture.

Hat was curious, as all Indians were inclined to be. Now he was wondering if the man with the new boots knew about the other water holes. Which side of the Pinacate would he take? He had an idea it would be the eastern side, away from the volcanic vents and the lava of the western slope.

Hat now had eleven warriors with him, all eager for the hunt. Four were Yaquis, one an outlaw Pima, and the others of the Yuma tribe. All but one had ridden with him before, although at different times.

With such a number he could herd the escaped prisoners like sheep, firing a bullet when necessary to turn them back, edging them away from the easiest routes, winning his final victory and the gold merely for a long ride into the desert. It amused Hat to consider that. Yet he had a moment of doubt. . . . There was that one with the new boots . . . he was a cunning traveler, like a prairie wolf. Would he find another way?

But eventually he must turn to the dunes. Of course, if he held to the line of mountains he could reach a point where the ride to the water would be shorter. If he tried that, they must head him off.

Hat was first of all a hunter, and as such, he was interested in what his prey might attempt. He was not worried. After all, they were amateurs in the Pinacate country; he was the professional. One last reservation he had . . . the Pinacate itself might take a hand in the game.

The old gods lurked among the mountains, this he knew, and the Pinacate was a place of the gods, as all such solitary places are apt to be. The Pinacate had moods and whims—sudden storms, strange fogs moving up from the Gulf, white frosts that came suddenly, even in summer. Such frosts appeared on the rocks in the morning and vanished with the first sun.

Directly in the path of the way they must go lay a forest of cholla. By appearing on the slopes to the east or west, he would herd his quarry into the cholla. Possibly they might pass through without injury, but such a thing rarely happened. There were paths that led into the cholla, some of which went nowhere, and he had made a few of these himself. On his various forays into the desert he would take the time to follow these little trails, in and out. Each was a cul-de-sac, a trap difficult to escape from without injury.

He had found these blind trails successful in putting his enemies afoot. A horse badly stabbed by the thorns of the cholla was a crippled horse. Hat had no such feeling for horses as was found among the Plains Indians, and also among some of his own tribe. To Hat the horse was something to ride, and when a horse died or was crippled, he got another one.

Finally Hat went to sleep. He would awaken with the first light, and that would be soon enough. It was up to him to choose the place where they would die, and in his own mind he had already made a selection.

Out on the lava, a coyote howled. A nighthawk swooped and darted in the night, and out on the broken basaltic fragments a tiny rock fell, rolled down a slope, and fell again.

The stars, like far-off campfires, held their stillness in the sky.

Tom Badger came out from the camp and paused beside Rodelo. "Quiet?"

"Yeah."

"Dan, you keep shy of Harbin. What's between you is your own business, and you settle it when you can, but now we're needin' every gun."

"I don't want to fight."

"You know, I'm wonderin' about you, Rodelo. Why are you here—what are you after?"

Rodelo ignored the question. He nodded his head toward the mountains. "You're an Indian, Tom . . . or part Indian. What's he waiting for?"

"The right time, the right place. He knows where we have to go, he knows how we have to get there."

Tom was silent for a moment. "I'd guess he only plans to kill one man."

"One?"

"Yeah . . . the last one."

CHAPTER 9

THE LAST STARS were still bright in the sky when they saddled up. The clumps of cholla seemed to glow with a light of their own, and the bleak moonscape of broken lava, eroded and faulted into a fantastic jumble of jagged rock, had an eerie look.

All of them were silent. There were only the sounds of leather creaking as saddles were heaved into place, of cinches tightened or packs adjusted.

The pack horses were in the worst shape. The gold was a load of about a hundred pounds, but it sat heavily, with none of the resilience of a live weight.

Rodelo, standing behind his horse, checked his gun. All the loads were in place, and he was ready. He holstered the gun but loosened the thong that held it in place, so it could be quickly removed.

Nora was first in the saddle. The others followed quickly, and after a moment in which no one moved Rodelo rode out, leading the way. He went eastward, then south, following the vestige of a trail that soon seemed to play out, but he held a course that could swing wide of Pinacate. Harbin came up beside him. "Where d'you think you're going?" he asked.

"If you want to try it due south, you go ahead. I'm riding around."

"What's down there?"

"There's a big crater. Between that crater and Pinacate Peaks there's the worst mess of pressure ridges and broken lava you'll ever see. Maybe there's a way through, but if there is I never saw it, and I'm not hunting it in the dark."

Grumbling, Harbin fell back. He was suspicious of every move Rodelo made, and his suspicions were growing stronger. He was operating with a short fuse, and the blow-off could come at any time.

Rodelo picked up the dim trail, skirted a shoulder of black basalt, and rode down into a crack, emerging in a forest of cholla. He drew up, his eyes scouting what lay ahead to be sure he got the trail. There were numerous openings, but none of them looked good. Finally he made a choice, but he moved slowly, avoiding the thick clumps of cholla. The wickedly barbed spines had a way of penetrating deeper if not removed, and they could cause painful sores.

Nobody was talking. They had no idea of how close the Yaquis might be, but voices carried far in the rocky desert, and they had no wish to be heard.

Before leaving the tanks, Rodelo had taken a long drink of water, and then had drunk again. Standing beside Nora, he had said, "An old desert Indian told me once that the water a man lost went from his blood first. Did you notice how little we bleed after a scratch? That must be the reason. And if that's true, it would slow up a man's actions and probably his thinking.

"A white man usually tries to ration his water, but an Indian drinks all he can hold whenever he gets a chance, knowing he will last longer, and be in better shape."

So far they had suffered little, but there had been a steady loss of water over the past few days which could have been only partly replaced by their drinking at the tanks. Watching, he had seen none of the others drink as much as he had.

When they came to a small clearing among the cholla, they drew up. Badger rode up to Rodelo. "Dan, we got a lame horse—a pack horse," he said.

Rodelo and the others gathered around. A joint of cholla was tightly caught in the horse's flesh just above the hock. There were thorns around the hoof, and flecks of blood on the shoulder.

"We'll have to turn him loose," Rodelo said. "We'll load the pack on the other horse, and split up the grub among us."

"Will he die?" Nora asked.

"Him? He's better off than we are. He'll have a sore leg and shoulder for a few days, but he will limp back to the tanks. There's water enough there for him."

"What will he eat?"

"What he ate last night. What the bighorns eat. Galleta grass, palo verde . . . he'll make out."

While the others stripped the pack from him, Rodelo extracted the thorns one by one, then released the horse with a slap on the hip. With only a few minutes' loss of time, they moved on, but now it was light.

Under ordinary conditions the horse crippled by cholla would soon have recovered, and had there been no demand for speed he could have been taken along. The pain caused by the stabbing of a cholla thorn is intense, and the joints of cholla are difficult to remove. Rodelo had found the simplest way was to put a knife blade or strong stick between the cholla joint and the part it had penetrated, and then with a quick jerk rip the thorn free. Some might stay in the skin, to be removed by the teeth if no tweezers were handy.

The Indians were not following them now. Knowing how their quarry must go, Hat led his band in a wide sweep to the playa beyond the edge of the lava, leaving one Indian to keep them in sight.

The sun rose above the horizon, and at once the rocks turned to flame and the desert shimmered with heat waves and mirage.

Dan Rodelo felt the sweat start to trickle down his face, and down his chest beneath his shirt. He rode with caution, not only because of the Indians but because of the desert itself. He guided his horse with care, choosing the ground over which they must go, not by miles but by yards, selecting each bit of route through the cholla, the ocotillo, and the jagged rocks.

Everything in the desert seems to wear a thorn; every plant, every living creature is equipped to survive in that most ruthless of all worlds. In the desert one quickly learned to stay on the sunny side of bushes, for a rattler might be coiled in the shade; one learned to avoid slippery rock, to be careful of the steep slides, to avoid if possible the deep stretches of sand that with each step robbed a man of his strength.

Now, Rodelo realized, the battle would soon be resolved. Within a matter of hours each man here would be in a deadly struggle merely to stay alive, and each was aware of it. The margin between life and death had narrowed here; a horse with a broken leg could put a man afoot, and from there there would be no escape. Without water, a man might, with luck, last twenty-four hours. A few, through sheer will to survive, had lasted three or four days.

"Watch yourself," Rodelo warned Nora. "If you bump

into a cholla bush you'll have a dozen or more thorns stuck into you, and every one hurting like the very devil."

Now there could be no question of speed. At times the trail was steep, and always it wound about among the cactus and the corners of jagged rock. The slightest slip meant falling against the thorns or the sharp rock edges.

Twice they stopped while Rodelo, not liking the looks of some opening ahead, would get down and explore on foot. It was a caution that paid off, for both openings were false leads.

Harbin was surly, his eyes scanning the rocks, but flickering over to Rodelo from time to time. Nora stayed close to Rodelo, and the gunman's jealousy grew. Tom Badger, with a gift for survival, stayed out of the line of fire and had no comments to make.

Starting up a slight incline in the lava maze, Gopher's mount suddenly slipped and fell back, throwing Gopher against a wall of cactus. The horse, fighting to his feet, was studded with cholla thorns; Gopher crawled out on his hands and knees, his back and side covered with the yellow joints.

Harbin burst out angrily, "You clumsy fool! Get yourself out of this! I'm going on!"

"We're all in this together," Rodelo said, "and we'll stick together."

"Who says so?" Harbin flared.

"I do," Rodelo replied.

There was a moment of silence. Harbin drew his horse around so that his right side was toward Rodelo. Harbin's hand was on his gun. "It ain't so far to the coast," he said. "You won't be needed."

Dan Rodelo was on the ground near Gopher, his knife

in his left hand. He was wondering how accurate a throw he could make. He could draw a gun or throw a knife with either hand, but a year in prison had given him no practice.

The bullet came an instant before the report, the smack of the bullet and the sound of the shot tripping over each other. All of them could hear the trickle of water as it ran from the canteen.

"You'll need me," Rodelo said. "You're going to be out of water."

Harbin swore, watching the last drops from the canteen dribble to the ground.

Rodelo went to work with his knife, first removing the cholla joints from Gopher then from the horse. Badger got down from his horse to help. Nora and Gopher held the horse while Rodelo, with Badger's help, extracted the thorns. The horse, ordinarily half-wild, seemed to know they were trying to help, and stood quietly. It cost them almost an hour.

"Let's get out of here," Rodelo said when the last joint had been pried loose. He started into a gap in the cactus growth, and a bullet clipped a joint of cholla behind him. They could see no one anywhere, and after a moment or so they went on.

In the dreadful heat, they could move only at the slowest pace. On their left several volcanic cones reared their heads. "Must be a hundred volcanoes in there," Gopher commented. "I never seen so many."

"Brady figured close to five hundred craters," Rodelo said. "He was down here some years back and knew the country as well as anybody."

The lava was a chaos of tilted blocks and pressure ridges, pock-marked with pits and deeper depressions;

old flows of lava were covered by later ones. The cactus grew everywhere, seeming to need no soil.

By midday they had gained very little distance. Once a wrong turning had led them into a dead-end canyon and they had been forced to retrace their steps. Finally they found a way out of the arroyo in which they had seemed trapped; but climbing the steep trail, a horse slipped and scraped his leg.

At one time they rode for an hour over thick volcanic ash—black, powdery dust that rose all around them and settled on their faces and clothing. They crossed a point of ropy lava and worked a precarious way among the small calderas, or craters. Twice they dismounted to walk, sparing their mounts as much as possible.

They plodded on in sullen silence, submitting to the heat like beaten slaves no longer possessing even the will to protest.

Once a lizard darted across the trail before them, but nothing else moved. They saw no bighorns, no javelinas, not even a rattlesnake. Several times they saw or believed they saw Indians, but there were no more shots.

The earth shimmered with heat waves; the distant mountains seemed nearer. Pools of water seemed to lie across their way just ahead of them, and once when they topped out on a ridge they saw a far-off playa that appeared to be one vast lake.

"Mirage," Badger said.

Their lips were cracked now, their mouths and throats parched. All of them were conscious of the slosh of water in the remaining canteen.

With startling suddenness they emerged from the chaos of lava and rode out upon a flat plain dotted with clumps of chamiso and creosote. No longer bunched together, they stretched out over at least a hundred yards, with Nora and Gopher bringing up the rear, separated by only a few yards.

The dead silence of the desert afternoon was split by the sharp reports of rifles. A bullet kicked dust just beyond the hoofs of Rodelo's horse. He drew swiftly and fired a shot that ricocheted off a rock slab. Behind him he heard a choking scream, and he turned his horse swiftly. The others were on a dead run for the cover of the rocks, but Gopher was down, and he was dead. Riding past him, Rodelo saw he had been hit at least twice, in the head and in the neck. The other pack horse was down.

Rodelo was in the open, facing toward the danger, expecting every moment to be fired on, but he could see nothing of the Yaquis.

The gold was there in that pack on the horse that was dead, but Gopher's horse was alive, if still in poor shape because of the bad fall into the cholla.

Now it was already the middle of the afternoon. How far had they come? Four or five miles? Perhaps even less. And now Gopher was gone.

Gopher was gone, a good horse was gone, and a canteen was gone.

Rodelo caught up Gopher's horse and stripped the saddle from it. He was strapping on the pack saddle when Badger and Harbin came out of the rocks, followed by Nora. They helped him hoist the gold into the saddle.

Badger turned to where Gopher lay. "You're forgettin' somethin', Joe." From Gopher's pocket he took the twenty-dollar gold pieces. "No use leaving that for those Injuns."

"Toss 'em once, for luck," Joe suggested.

Badger flipped the coins in the air and Joe promptly grabbed them before Badger could. "Thanks, sucker," he said with a grin.

Tom Badger stood very still, looking at him, his eyes utterly cold. Then he walked to his horse.

Rodelo handed the remaining canteen to Nora. "Drink," he said.

"I can manage."

"Go ahead," Badger agreed. "You drink it, lady."

She glanced at Harbin. "Sure," he said. "I want to keep you alive."

She took a swallow, then passed it to Rodelo. He handed it on to Badger. When it was returned to him there was barely a swallow of lukewarm water, but it seemed amazingly cool to his parched mouth.

"Throw it away," Harbin said. "I don't like the empty sound of it."

"And if we find a water hole? What will we carry water in? Nobody in his right mind ever threw a canteen away in the desert."

"That reminds me," Badger said, "that this lady said she knew of a water hole. Or have you forgot?"

"I say we make a run for the coast," Harbin said. "How much farther can it be?"

"Too far," Rodelo replied.

"You say it's too far, but what if we waste time looking for water and don't find any?"

"The breaks of the game," Rodelo said shortly.

Badger looked at Nora. "Do you know where there's water?"

"The water hole I know of is at the south end of the Pinacate."

"That's near where we are now."

Nothing more was said, and they moved on. Dan Rodelo was in the lead again, just ahead of Nora. "Do you know any landmarks?" he asked her. "How do we know where this place is?"

"I will know it . . . I think."

He glanced back at her in amazement. "You've actually been in this country?"

"When I was a child."

Suddenly he turned in the saddle. "Then you must be Nora Reilly!"

"What do you know about Nora Reilly?" she asked.

"Shipwreck on the Gulf . . . eighteen or nineteen years ago. Small sailer of some kind, headed for Yuma. She got caught in the tidal bore . . . on the edge of it, I guess. Smashed into some rocks, but they got ashore, and they made it overland to Sonoyta—a little border town up yonder."

She nodded her head, but said nothing.

He rode on. Suddenly he saw some broken pottery, rusty brown in color, and crudely made. He drew up, then walked his horse around slowly. At one place the rocks seemed to have a whitish streak across them . . . it was the vestige of an ancient trail.

He walked his horse along the trail. Here was more broken pottery, and an olla, a pot used to hold water. Then he rode out on a ledge and looked down at a tank . . . it was bone-dry.

"There should be water," Badger said hoarsely. "There's been rain."

Rodelo pointed. A slab of rock had fallen across the channel that fed water into the tank. The run-off had plunged off down the slope and lost itself in the sand. He got down and went to the rock. It took some tugging to move it, but finally he got it loose and moved it to one side. Neither of the other men offered to help.

"Why waste time?" Harbin asked. "We ain't comin' this way again."

"Somebody else may."

Rodelo got back in the saddle. The struggle with the rock had left him exhausted, and it warned him of how narrow was the margin of strength left to him.

They had now been on short water since just after leaving Papago Tanks. They had been riding and walking in blazing sun. By now their blood would be thickening, their responses slowing down.

But when they passed the olla he reached down and picked it up, holding it before him on the saddle. It would hold a good deal of water . . . if they ever found any.

CHAPTER 10

THERE WAS NO shield from the sun. Nowhere a cloud, nor even a shadow. They plodded along wearily, slumping in their saddles, drained of energy by the fierce heat. When they lifted their heads to look about, even their eyeballs moved sluggishly, the movements of their hands felt awkward.

Dan Rodelo pulled up and slid from the saddle. By all means, he must save the *grulla*. The mouse-colored mustang might be all that he had between himself and death, and they would need each other.

The Yaquis did not worry them just now. Perhaps in the maze of rocks behind them their trail had been temporarily lost. None of them expected anything more than that.

Nobody talked of water. Nobody wanted to think of it, and yet they thought of nothing else.

Nora spoke suddenly. "There! I think it is there!"

She pointed toward three identical sahuaros that lifted their tall columns from a point of rock, standing close together like three upraised fingers.

There was no rush to seek the water, for their fear of disappointment was too great. Rodelo left his horse and climbed among the rocks. He heard the buzzing of bees, and turned left to follow the sound. He slipped on the lava, caught himself on his hand as he fell, and got clumsily to his feet, then looked stupidly at his bloody, lacerated palm.

Clinging to a rock to steady himself, he edged around a corner and looked upon a wide, shallow pool of water. At one side, where a trail came in, there was a flat surface and a small edge of sand. At the far side of the pool the water became deeper.

He walked back to his horse. "It's there," he said, "enough to fill our canteen and water the horses, and drink what we want."

He motioned them around to the trail so they could bring the horses up. Then he took the olla and went back to the pool. He went to the deepest part, filled the olla, and placed it back in a shadowed corner where a shelf of rock would protect it from the sun. When the others came up, he was drinking deeply at the basin's edge.

"Hold the horses back," Harbin said. "Let's get our water before they stir it up."

Badger filled the canteen before he drank. While Nora was drinking, Rodelo looked around. This was a sheltered spot, a place that could be guarded, and defended. And there was some shade against the late afternoon sun. "Let's camp right here," he said.

Tom Badger glanced over at Joe Harbin before replying. "Might as well," he agreed. "We ain't likely to find a better place."

They brought the horses in and watered them, then led them to the shadows under the basaltic rim that partly enclosed the basin. The horses needed the rest . . . they all did.

"There's enough dry wood for a fire. That stuff won't send up any smoke," Badger said.

"All right," Rodelo agreed.

Westward, and within plain view from where they stood, were the dunes, the great wall of dunes at least five miles across that separated them from the somewhat harder surface along the shore of the Gulf of California. Southwest was the short range of jagged mountains, the Sierra Blanca, already partly buried in the drifting sand.

Dan Rodelo looked at those dunes and swore softly to himself. He hated the thought of attempting to cross them tomorrow. All of them were already exhausted, and the horses had given all they could. The heat and the shortage of water had sapped their strength and their powers of endurance to the limit. And somewhere not far off were the Indians.

Somehow, he was sure, they had evaded the Yaquis for the moment. By some accidental twist and turn they had slipped off and left the Indians following along in another direction. Not that it would give them more than a few hours leeway. Without doubt the Indians had scouts out searching for them even now.

There had been no horse tracks or human tracks around this tank, and that meant it was either unknown to the Yaquis or unused by them. Perhaps the tank was normally empty at this season, but even so, had it been used at times the tracks would have been there. And the only ones he had seen were those of bighorn sheep and the odd twisting trail of a sidewinder.

Dan Rodelo stared off toward the dunes, but he was keeping Badger and Harbin within view at all times. From now on he must be wary, for he was sure neither of them had any plan to share the gold with him. As soon as the danger of Indian attack seemed past, they would waste no more time.

Nora moved over to stand beside him. Her lips were

cracked, her cheeks burned red along the cheekbones, but nothing could spoil completely the quiet beauty of her face.

"I love the desert at this hour," she said, as she looked westward. "I like to see the shadows gather, and feel the coolness come."

"Enjoy it while you can. Tomorrow will be our worst day."

"I think so too. I can remember the sand dunes."

"I wonder that you survived. That must have been a tough trek for a youngster."

"It wasn't that. It was what I'd left behind. I lost my family in that wreck. At least, I lost all of it I knew." She looked at him suddenly. "You see, I don't even know who I am, or where I came from. My father was drowned over there in the Gulf, my mother died in the desert just at the edge of the dunes, only a few miles from here."

"Dean Stafford brought you across the desert. Five of you started, and three of you made it across. I heard the story."

Rodelo paused a moment. "What I don't understand is why you ever wanted to come back."

"I was alone in the world, and I did not want to be alone. I . . . I wanted to find something, something we left back there."

"You left a lot back there, Nora. You left a father and a mother, but you cannot find them now. It is too late for that."

"Maybe it isn't."

He turned to face her questioningly. "Nora . . ."

"You do not understand. We *did* leave something back there . . . a box."

"A *box*?"

"Oh, it was nothing much. Just some things my mother loved. Some letters, some pictures . . . nothing valuable. At least, nothing valuable to anybody but me. But don't you see? In a way those things *are* me.

"I was too young to really know either my father or mother, but if I could see their pictures, read some letters they wrote, maybe I could make them seem real to me. I have been thinking of this ever since I was a little girl, because if I have these things that belonged to them, in a certain sense I will have *them*. They won't be just shadowy figures I can only vaguely remember, but real people, my people, my family. My own father and mother."

"You risked *this*, for *that*?"

"I know what you're thinking. It is what everyone thought when I said I wanted to come down here, but don't you see? I've never had anyone who was really my own. I had foster parents and they were good to me; and after they died I finished school on the money they left me, but always I kept thinking of this place. I had to come back. I simply must find that box."

"I never had any idea what was pushing you." He hesitated. "Do you really think it is wise? Suppose you found . . . well, suppose you found they weren't what you would have wished them to be? Sometimes it is better to have the dream than the reality."

"I've thought of that. No . . . I must find out. I must know. Why, I don't even know where they were coming from or where they were going . . . or why."

It was a question that had puzzled Rodelo. If Dean Stafford, whom he had known slightly, had any idea who Nora Reilly's parents were he had never said. Rodelo thought back. Dean had rarely talked about that trek across the Pinacate country . . . not that Stafford had been a taciturn man, for he was not. There simply had not been much to tell. He had told Rodelo about the water holes . . . as much as he knew.

Rodelo knew all that anyone had known. The outfit had started for Yuma, on the Colorado River. Stafford knew they were on some sort of a sailing craft. What he knew about ships could have been written on a postage stamp, as he often said. On board ship he had never talked to the child Nora nor to her parents. They had kept to themselves, were well dressed, polite, but somewhat stand-offish.

The boat's captain was no sailor. He was headed for the goldfields at Ehrenberg, and had bought the boat to get passage to the mouth of the river. Caught in the tidal bore, he had never even known what hit him, nor did Stafford until he reached Yuma. When the child's mother died she asked Stafford to see that her child was cared for.

Who came to Yuma in those days? Who was headed upriver? Gamblers, honky-tonk girls, miners, adventurers . . . occasionally soldiers bound for one of the inland forts. Knowing who came up the river then, Rodelo would gamble that the odds were five to one neither of her parents was any good. They were probably people who followed the mining camps for whatever they could get in whatever way was possible in a rough camp among rough men.

Suddenly Harbin was beside them. "What are you two talkin' about? Rodelo, don't you forget this here's my girl."

"Your girl?" Nora turned on him. "Why, Mr. Harbin! Whatever gave you that idea? I wasn't aware that I was anybody's girl."

He looked hard at her. "Lady, out here you got no choice."

"I think she has," Rodelo said.

Harbin ignored Rodelo's remark. "Look, lady, you better make up your mind. We ain't got far to go. I can take you on with me, or I can leave you down there on the coast, whichever you like."

Dan Rodelo smiled at him. "Joe, you never could see much farther than your nose; but if you can't, Tom Badger can. Sam Burrows, back there in the States, he knows this girl left with us. If she doesn't show up, he's going to ask questions."

"What do I care? I ain't never comin' back."

"Tom," Rodelo said, "tell Joe about Kosterlitzky."

"What about him?" Badger asked.

"Sam Burrows has two good friends in the world, Tom. Oh, he has many friends, but he has two almighty good friends, and one of them is Emilio Kosterlitzky, who commands the Rurales. I think you boys have heard of them?

"Well," he went on, "if Sam suggested to Emilio that he would like to know what became of Nora Paxton, Emilio would find whoever traveled with her and he'd make them sweat a little and bleed a little and suffer a whole lot until they told. And if the news was bad news, Emilio would just naturally feel that he had to send something to Sam Burrows to show his friendship, something like scalps, for instance. I'm not saying he would literally collect your scalps, but what he would send back would be evidence enough."

"You don't scare me."

"He does me," Badger said. "That Kosterlitzky is pure hell."

Neither of the men said any more, and they turned away.

There was dead mesquite near the water hole, and enough dry wood to make a small fire, sheltered from observation. The coffee tasted good, and they had the last of the jerked beef from Sam Burrows' store.

Rodelo stayed back from the fire, eating in silence, listening for sounds from outside the basin. He had no confidence in their escape from the Indians. If by some luck they had evaded the Indians, it could not be for long. There would be a fight, sooner or later.

"We'd better graze the horses," Badger suggested. "There's mesquite outside the bowl."

"I noticed some grass there," Nora said.

The horses needed it. These past few days had been cruelly hard for both man and beast, but horses could not stand what a man could, and if there was any forage they should have it.

It was Joe Harbin who led them out and picketed them on the galleta grass near the mesquite. Rodelo was careful to be watching when he returned . . . he wanted no sudden shot, no advantage given to Harbin, who needed none.

Now that the last hours were coming, Rodelo had no plan. He could only go ahead, let them do what they might. One thing he did know, he was not going to allow that gold to be taken away from him.

His thoughts went to Nora. Was there more in that box than she admitted? Treasure, perhaps? It was unlikely, and no matter how absurd her reasons might seem to others, he could understand them. In these days a girl with no family, no background, no money had little chance. Work that decent women could do was strictly limited by custom; but everywhere women were asked who they were, from what family they came, what was their background. The West did not ask questions of its men, but it still wanted to know about its women.

Aside from that, what meant so much to Nora was just the knowing. He had been through it himself, and he still bore the scars of not knowing anything of his family. She had courage, this girl did. How many women would have dared the desert in the company of such men as these?

As he looked to the west, he saw far off a blue line of mountains in Baja California, across the Gulf. The sun was setting beyond them now, and was leaving a painted sky behind. Coolness was coming to the desert. Rodelo leaned back against the rock wall, half propped up by his saddle. He was tired . . . tired.

He wanted another cup of coffee, but lacked the energy to get up and get it. For several minutes he sat looking at the pot and measuring his weariness against the desire for the coffee. Then the realization that it might help on the following day, when every drop of moisture would count, won the argument.

He leaned forward to get up and the bullet smashed into the rock where his head had been, spattering him with stinging rock fragments. He threw himself to the ground, drawing as he went down, and in that split second he glimpsed the face of an Indian. He fired . . . missed . . . the face vanished.

With a lunge, he was across the basin and scrambling around the rocks. He heard the Indian yelling, trying to stampede the horses. For a moment then, he caught sight of him, and fired again.

The light was vague, and the Indian was sixty feet off,

but the bullet caught him in the top of the head, killing him instantly.

A voice spoke at his elbow. "Now that's what I call shootin'," Badger said. "I didn't figure you were that good."

"Lucky," Harbin said. "A scratch shot."

"You've got to buy chips to find out, Joe," Dan said quietly. "You've got to stack your bet."

Harbin also had his gun in his hand. "When I'm ready," he said, "you'll draw to a busted flush. And you'll get three aces . . . right through the belly."

"Forget it," Badger said shortly. "What about this Injun?"

"We'd better round up the horses first," Rodelo said.

"Don't worry about them," said Badger. "In the shape they're in and the way they're feelin', they won't go far. Not while there's water in this hole."

He went on, "I figure this Injun was a scout who located us. He aimed to set us afoot and make the rest of it easy whilst he sent up a smoke to bring the others around."

"Now that's a thought," Dan said.

"You mean to send up a smoke?"

"Sure . . . from where we aren't. Like that notch over there."

"If it works," Harbin agreed, "we could gain five or ten miles on them. We might get off scot-free." He hesitated. "Who sends up the smoke?"

"And why that notch?" Badger asked. "Why should they expect us to be over there?"

"That's the best trail to the coast. If they see a smoke go up from there they'll believe it."

"I like it," Badger acknowledged. "It might work."

"Okay, Tom," Harbin said. "You like it so much, you ride over and send up the smoke."

"And meet those Indians all by myself?"

"You scared?"

"You bet I am. I want no part of those boys. They're not like my kind of Indians. I'm as scared of them as you are."

"I'll go," Rodelo said evenly.

"Then you'd better get started." Joe Harbin gave him a taunting smile. "Those Injuns will be expectin' that signal."

Rodelo walked to the *grulla,* led it into the basin, and saddled up. As he tightened the cinch he was thinking of the situation. It had to resolve itself quickly now. The beach was just over there across the dunes, and he did not want to precipitate a gun battle if he could help it. But when he told them he was taking the gold back, all hell would break loose . . . unless they risked shooting him first.

Nora Paxton came close to him. "Don't go, Dan."

"Someone has to."

"Why not Tom or Joe?"

"With all that gold at stake they won't risk turning their backs on each other. This is a last man's club, Nora, and I have to be the last man."

"Why, Dan? Is the money so important to you?"

"Yes, it is. Right now I'd say that money means more to me than anything else in the world."

"More than I do?"

He looked down at her. "Yes, Nora, right now it means more than you do. If it did not mean so much, you could not mean so much to me. It is a matter of honor."

She drew back from him. "Pride, maybe—not honor.

Well, that shows me where I stand." She turned away sharply and walked off.

"Nora!"

She ignored him, and went to the fire. For a moment he stood staring after her, wanting to say more, yet afraid to show his hand, afraid of being overheard. Harbin was already suspicious, and as for Tom Badger, a man never knew about Badger. He played his cards close to his vest and nobody ever knew what he was holding.

Rodelo led his horse to the trail out of the basin. Joe Harbin followed after him, then Badger. Nora remained where she was, beside the fire.

"Where do you figure we should go from here?" Badger asked.

"West. Keep the Sierra Blanca on your left, and when you pass the point of that range, stay half a mile or so north of it. As you ride west, keep yourself lined up on the gap between Pinacate and the Sierra Blanca, and the coast you reach will be on Adair Bay."

"What about water?" Harbin asked. "On the bay, I mean?"

Dan Rodelo smiled at him. "Why, there's several springs down there . . . or water holes of some kind. Some of them are fresh water, some aren't. If you get there before I do, you just sit and wait. I'll be along to show you where the water is."

"What about you?"

"Me? I'll be riding north along the western line of Pinacate for a few miles. I'll just come back here for water. I won't need much."

He turned in the saddle and glanced toward the fire. Nora's back was turned toward him.

"*Adios!*" he called, and rode away.

Joe Harbin was grinning. Badger looked at him suspiciously. "What's so funny?"

"Him . . . he said he'd come back here for water. When he gets back there's not going to be any left."

"You'd dry it up?"

"The horses wil take most of it. What we can't take we'll just dry up. I think we've seen the last of Dan Rodelo."

Tom Badger looked thoughtfully after the vanishing rider. "Yeah," he said doubtfully, "it looks that way."

Nora, standing by the fire, was shading her eyes toward the west, watching him go.

CHAPTER 11

RODELO RODE WEST, and then north. And from the moment of leaving the water hole he believed he was followed. Of course, that might simply come from the feeling the desert could give. At the same time, he had the sensation of being almost naked, exposed to view from all sides.

He rode with his Winchester in his hand, his eyes never ceasing their movement, studying every corner and crack in the lava, studying the ground for tracks.

The first sign was scarcely a track. A piece of black rock no larger than his fist had been knocked from its usual resting place. The desert rocks wear desert polish on their surface, that patina or finish applied to exposed rock by the desert sun, the wind, the rain, and the blown sand, and perhaps by chemical actions within itself.

This rock showed that it had been turned on its side, and what had been the top was now half buried in the sand. A man or an animal, leaping from rock to rock, might have dragged his toe at that point. It was an indication that something had passed by there, and therefore it was a warning.

Rodelo rode warily through a clump of cholla, paused briefly in the partial shadow of a giant sahuaro, then moved out. The point for which he was heading was not far off.

By now Badger, Harbin, and Nora would be starting

into the sand hills. There a walking man could sink halfway to his knees at every step, or slide back one step for every two steps forward. A horse could sink in to its belly if it was carrying a rider. Once in the sand dunes, they would lose sight of Pinacate, their only landmark. From time to time they might see it, but unless they were especially careful they could spend time and effort struggling against the sand in the wrong direction. To maintain a true course there would be a part of the difficulty.

Now he saw, off to his right and close against the base of the mountain, a clump of mesquite—perhaps eight or ten good-sized trees—and a sahuaro and some cholla grew nearby. The clump of mesquite would be an ideal place to leave his *grulla*.

The mouse-colored horse was in better shape than the others. In any event he was a good horse, a mustang born to desert and mountains, used to getting along on sparse water and the indifferent forage supplied by the desert. That horse was Dan Rodelo's ace in the hole, for he knew that when the chips were down the mustang would stand up long after the strength of the other horses had failed. This it was that would save him from the desert.

Once among the mesquite, he stepped down from the saddle and tied the *grulla*. The horse would feed off the green leaves and the beans while he was gone. Taking his rifle, he left the cluster of mesquite and scrambled up the steep side of the mountain toward the notch.

A few hundred yards off, a Yaqui drew up and watched for a moment. Then he slid off his horse, tied it, and started up a game trail. He had known where the trail was, and had waited to see if Rodelo planned what he expected, and then he took his own route to the top. Following a trail known to him, he could move faster and more easily than the white man.

The Indian's dark eyes gleamed with anticipation . . . this was the one with the boots that Hat had spoken of. He was also the one who knew the water holes and who was a great warrior. To bring his body back and to claim the reward would be something to boast of in the lodges of his people.

He had no doubt about it—the white man was climbing to his death.

When Dan Rodelo reached the notch, he found it in no way extraordinary. He saw a game trail coming in from the south that would have made his climb easier had he known of it. There was some cholla there at the notch, a half-dead palo verde, and some flimsy skeletons of dead cacti.

Gathering these together with some dead burro bush and a few fragments of the palo verde, he struck a match. The slight wind puffed it out. He stood his Winchester against a rock and dug for another match. Crouching, he turned his head and searched the rocks carefully. He was in a sort of basin formed by the notch. On the east he could catch a glimpse of the chaos of lava below the mountain, on the left were the dunes; and far off, the shimmer of sunlight on the Gulf. He felt uneasy, but he bunched his kindling and was about to strike the second match.

Behind him something brushed faintly on rock. Turning, as if to pick up another stick, he glanced over his shoulder. A lizard lay upon the flat surface of a rock, its little sides panting. He watched it a moment without moving. Had the lizard made the sound? Suddenly, its head went up and it was gone like a streak across the sand.

First, the smoke. His ears pricked for the slightest sound, he struck the match and touched it to the dead leaves and branches. A thin tendril of smoke started to rise. He added more fuel, and then, at a whisper of sound behind him, he threw himself to one side.

The Yaqui landed on the balls of his feet where a moment before Rodelo had crouched. Instantly, Rodelo kicked out with both feet, staggering the Indian. Springing up, he was ready when the Indian turned on him and sprang in with knife held low.

Dan slapped the knife wrist aside, grasped it with his other hand and, thrusting a leg across in front of the Indian, broke him over it to the ground, twisting the knife from his grip. The knife fell to the sand and the Indian, slippery as a snake, slid from his grasp and was up. Rodelo feinted as the Indian lunged, and sent a right at him coming in.

The Indian stopped in mid-stride, and Dan, too anxious, missed his punch and fell against him. Both went to the ground. The Yaqui was quicker, whipping over Dan and thrusting a forearm across his throat.

Rodelo was down on his back, the arm across his throat, when the Indian reached for a grip on his throat with the other hand. Dan swung his feet high and caught both heels across the warrior's face, raking him with a spur and bending him backwards off his body. Dan came up, gasping for breath, his throat bruised.

The Yaqui squirmed away, then leaped up, blood running from his face, gashed by the spur. He circled warily, swept up his knife, and lunged at Dan again, who threw himself aside, tripping the Indian. The Yaqui came up again, thrust with the knife and ripped Dan's sleeve. Then Dan moved in, watching his chance. He dared not use his gun, for there might be other Indians near. His own knife was at his belt, a thong around it. His hand went to the knife, reaching for the thong.

A swift slash with the Yaqui's knife ripped Dan's shirt across the front and he felt the sting of the cut across his hard-muscled stomach. But the slash with the knife had swung the Indian around, and Dan kicked him on the knee. Before he could recover, Rodelo rushed in, heaved him bodily from the ground, and threw him into a patch of cholla.

The Indian screamed, and struggled to get free, but with each movement he picked up more joints of cholla. His struggling only served to get him into a worse condition. Rodelo backed off and picked up his rifle.

The smoke was climbing to the sky now in a thin column. Adding fuel, Dan looked over at the suffering Indian. "You asked for it, boy," he said grimly. "Now you get out of it."

He left at once, starting down through the rocks at a breakneck clip. The Yaquis would be coming, and he had no idea how far away they were.

He was on a ledge almost at the bottom when he saw a rider with a led horse come out of the mesquite and start down the trail. It was Joe Harbin, and he was leading the *grulla*!

"Joe!" he yelled. "Joe!"

Harbin turned in his saddle, thumbed his nose at him, and kept going.

Furious, Rodelo whipped his rifle to his shoulder, but Harbin was already down in the arroyo and out of sight. When he appeared later he was out of range . . . at least beyond accurate shooting, and a miss might kill the *grulla*.

They had him now, as good as dead. He was without a horse, without water, and the Yaquis were coming nearer every moment. He had to move. Somehow he must get to water, he must cross the dunes, he must survive.

His heart beat heavily with apprehension. He knew the desert too well not to know his chances were slim. The jaunt back to the hidden olla with its water supply would have meant little on a horse. Afoot, it was a matter of life and death. And suppose they had found the olla and broken it?

He had to move, yet he did not immediately. From this moment, every step he made must be a step in the right direction. To move without thinking was to ask for death.

Tom Badger would lead the way through the dunes, and they would have started without Joe Harbin. By the time Joe caught up they would be well into the sand and would be having a bad time. Once in the sand, the horses would be of little use to them, and the two men and the girl would have a struggle with them to even get them through. And during that time the Indians would be moving upon them. A man on foot could move faster than a horse in the dunes.

Rodelo had already been several hours without a drink of water. He was, he believed, closer to the shore at this point than Badger and Nora were, but he could not be sure, and to be lost in the dunes would be fatal. He knew that from now on, he was walking a thin wire, with death on either hand.

He moved then, keeping to the heaviest growth, searching for the few shadows, working into the thickest clumps of brush. The first thing to do was to get away from the mountain, away from observation.

He went on, turning south presently, and walked at a steady pace, or as steady a pace as the terrain would permit. He was alert for trouble, and he felt good to be moving. Somewhere ahead of him the showdown awaited . . . and then, if lucky, the gold and Nora.

For the first hour the going was not too difficult, and he made good time . . . he went perhaps two and a half miles. The next hour was over lava, in and out of the edge of the dunes, and he made less than half that distance. Time and again he was tempted to turn directly into the dunes and try to fight his way through to the shore. There were places where the sand seemed well packed, but he could not depend on it, and he needed water desperately.

By now his mouth was dry, his lips parched, his tongue like a stick in his mouth. His pace had slowed noticeably, and his reactions were slow too. He fought the urge to discard his rifle. He saw no Indians.

It was sundown when he finally reached the tank. As he had expected, the others were gone; and as he had feared, his olla was broken . . . that would have been Joe Harbin. But there was a taste of water in the bottom, not more than a swallow and he drank it eagerly. The water in the tank was gone, every last drop.

One thing he did find—an abandoned canteen with a bullet hole through it. Suddenly a thought came to him, and he stripped the blanket covering from the canteen. Dew would form on metal.

He considered moving on, thought of the risks, and decided to wait here and rest. He lay down and tried to sleep, but his thirst kept him awake. Then he recalled seeing a good-sized barrel cactus above the tank. Cautiously, he made his way through the broken lava about the tank and found it. Wary of its spines, he managed to slice off the top. Reaching in, he got a handful of the pulp and squeezed the juice into his mouth. It was somewhat bitter, but it was wet. For what seemed like a long time, he kept dipping into the top of the barrel cactus and squeezing the drops into his mouth. When he lay down again, he slept.

He awakened suddenly, conscious of a penetrating chill. Going to the canteen, he licked the dew from the surface and felt better, little though it was.

He thought of the tank in the Sierra Blanca—with luck there would be water there. If he were to start for it at once, there was a fair chance he could make it shortly after daylight. . . . But suppose there was no water there? Then he would have to strike for the coast, with not a chance in a thousand of making it through.

By the time he had reached that conclusion he was walking, stepping out almost mechanically, his mind seemingly only half aware of what he was doing. On the horizon to the southwest he could see the ugly bulk of the Sierra, and the thought occurred to him that he should have struck out at once through the sand hills for the shore . . . back there where he had lost his horse. By now he might have been standing on the shore of the Gulf. . . .

He fell down.

Staggering, he got up, wary of rocks. Like a drunken man, he felt his way cautiously, uncertainly, and stepped out upon a level space and started walking fast—or so he thought.

After a while he was conscious that it was growing

light. He was dimly aware that he had fallen again . . . several times. And the mountains seemed no nearer.

He walked on, staggering and falling.

He was almost to the foot of the mountains when he fell again, and this time he could not get up.

He pulled one knee up and tried to roll up on it, but could not. He crawled a few feet on his belly, aware of the blistering heat of the sand. The thought went through his mind that if the air above was 120 degrees, it might be as much as 160 degrees down on the sand. But he could not get up. Yet he clung to the rifle, and to the canteen.

He had been lying there for some time when he realized he was staring at the side of a barrel cactus. The realization heaved him to his knees, and the rifle, used as a crutch, got him to his feet.

Fumbling with his knife, he got it out and slashed off the top of the barrel. Once again he squeezed moisture from the pulp into his mouth, a miracle of coolness that seemed to go all through him.

After a few minutes, he started on once more.

When he came to the tank in the Sierra Blanca he found that it was in a hollowed rock basin under a waterfall. The water was deep and cold.

CHAPTER 12

TOM BADGER WAS in the lead, and was starting to skirt a deep crater when they saw Harbin approaching, leading the *grulla*. Tom drew up. "Looks like Rodelo must have run into trouble," he said.

Nora's lips tightened, but she said nothing. Her heart was pounding as Harbin drew nearer, her body felt suddenly cold and stiff, as she had never felt before.

"What happened?" Badger asked.

"Looks like Danny's plan to draw Indians drew them faster than he figured."

"Tough."

"Well," Harbin said, "it wasn't my idea to send up that smoke."

"Nobody to blame but himself," Badger agreed. Then, for Nora's benefit, he added, "But he gave his life tryin' to help us."

"Where is he?" Nora's voice was cold.

"Dead, more'n likely. Them Indians ain't much on prisoners."

"Why would they want him? I mean when he wasn't with you? He isn't an escaped convict, and they couldn't get a dollar for him."

Badger glanced at Harbin and said, "He was with us. They knew it, and that would be enough. Come on, we're wastin' time."

Nora swung her mount. "I'm going back after him. A man like Dan Rodelo doesn't die that easy."

"Are you crazy?" Harbin almost shouted at her. "He wouldn't have a chance, back there. You wouldn't neither."

"Just the same, I am going back."

She started her horse and Harbin swung his alongside. "You are, like hell!" He reached over and slapped her across the mouth. "You're my woman, and you'd better know it! From now on you ain't goin' nowhere unless I tell you!"

"Let go of my horse."

Deliberately, he swung the horse around, and Nora, lifting her quirt, struck him hard across the face with it.

Wrenching it from her hand, he threw it onto the sand. The livid streak left by the lash lay across his face. There was blood on his lips where it had cut into the chapped flesh. Harbin's eyes were ugly.

"You'll pay for that, a-plenty. You ride along now. You may last out the year, but I won't never let you forget that blow, believe me. Now get on before I kill you right here."

He started her horse toward the dunes. "You might as well know it—I'm the boss man from here on."

Tom Badger pulled his horse alongside, and Joe reined in. "Ride on ahead, Tom," he said.

"You're the boss, you said."

"That's right. And I'll give the orders."

"Not in the back, Joe. I'm not Rodelo. We ride together."

Harbin shrugged. "Suits me, if you feel you're safer."

Skirting the crater, they picked their way across the broken lava, following a precarious trail. To the north a long dune stretched out far to the east, at one point coming almost to the base of the Pinacate. From time to time they glanced back to look for the gap between Pinacate and Sierra Blanca. Then they entered the dunes.

They had drunk well before leaving the tank, and if the horses held up they hoped to be through the dunes in two or three hours, or even less if they found a place where the sand was hard-packed. At one place they saw the raw granite peaks of a sand-buried mountain range projecting a few feet above the sand. The time would come when they would be completely covered, a range of mountains several hundred feet high drowned in the sand.

A huge dune lifted on their right, another on the left. They rode a few yards and then found their way partly blocked by a drift of sand several feet high. The horses plunged and struggled getting through it, and by the time they reached the small space beyond it they were blowing hard. Tom Badger swung down, his face gray.

"We got trouble," he said.

Harbin nodded. "Must be an easier way through." The dune ahead of them was at least sixty feet of slanting sand, not too steep, but soft.

"Maybe . . . but we ain't got the time to look for it."

They started on, struggling up the long slope of the dune, sinking over their ankles, the horses going in over their hocks. But they kept going, and made the top of the dune. Looking back, they could see the way they had come . . . not much more than a hundred yards.

Joe Harbin swore bitterly. He could have sworn they had walked almost a mile.

They pushed on, but it was an unending struggle. The horses lunged, the packs came loose. There was no question of riding; they not only had to lead their horses, but had to pull to help them through the sand.

There was a temptation, once on top of a dune, to follow its ridge. Once, finding a ridge that seemed to run in a somewhat southwesterly direction, they did follow it rather than descend into the hollow between that one and the next, a higher dune. When they looked back they had lost their guide mark, the gap between the mountains.

When perhaps an hour had passed, they stood together on the crest of a long sand hill. In no direction could they see anything but sand.

"I've got to rest," Harbin muttered. He dropped to the sand and put his head on his arms, which lay across his knees.

There was a faint breeze that smelled of the sea. Nora inhaled deeply, hoping it would last, but it did not. After a while they started on. There was no sign of pursuit.

Nora Paxton was a girl who had spent much of her life riding, canoeing, hiking in the woods, and she was glad of it now. Neither of the men had ever done much but ride a horse until they went to prison, and there was no question of even walking more than a few yards while guests of the Territory of Yuma.

Now she was thinking of Dan Rodelo. She told herself that what Harbin had said must be true. Dan was out there either dead or wandering on foot in the desert's heat. If he was not dead he soon would be.

For the first time she began to realize fully what might be the consequences of her longing to hold in her hands once more something that belonged to her mother. It was coming home to her that she might not extricate herself from the situation into which she had forced herself. Even if they got out of the dunes alive, which at this point was uncertain, there would remain the problem of escaping from Joe Harbin, and possibly from Tom Badger. If successful in that, she must still get back to civilization somehow.

During most of her life she had followed the way that seemed open at the time. Things had gone well for her, considering everything. But until now she had been dealing with civilized people in a civilized and ordered world. Now she might as well be a million miles away from that world.

She did not for a minute believe that Dan Rodelo had been dead when Joe Harbin took his horse. Or rather, she had believed it for no longer than a minute. Somehow Harbin had murdered Rodelo or had contrived to set him afoot—which was much the same thing.

Of one thing she was sure. She was in better shape to cope with the present situation than either man was. Both were riders, not walkers; both had spent some time in prison, a part of it in solitary confinement. They had been weakened by lack of exercise, inadequate food, and lack of the need for effort. The hard labor they had been doing during the past few days had only just begun.

She had to get away—somehow she must escape them. But what if the Indians came, as they were sure to do? Harbin and Badger must at least defend her as they must defend themselves. She would wait, at least until the Indians had attacked; and knowing the two men, she knew no Indian or anyone else was likely to take them easily.

They struggled on, falling down, tugging at the bridles, even pushing the horses. The packs slipped, were readjusted, slipped again.

Suddenly Badger stopped. "Joe . . . look!" He pointed

at the declining sun, and it was on their right. Still high in the sky, still blazing hot, but on their right. They were going south, not west!

Joe Harbin swore slowly, in a muffled, ugly tone.

His cheekbones were streaks of red from the sun. His cracked lips were white with dust, as was his beard. His cruel black eyes were deep-sunken under shaggy brows. Grimly, he turned right, descended a couple of hundred feet on a long slope of sand, then started up, at an angle, another long slope.

Twice they believed they had reached the edge of the dunes, but each time more sand hills lay beyond. Finally at sunset, from the crest of a dune, they saw the sea.

They stood unmoving, struck dumb at the sight. The sun was setting beyond the dark mountains of Baja California, but nearer to them lay that thin streak of blue that was the Gulf.

"We made it," Harbin croaked. "By the Lord Harry, we made it!"

"Not yet," Badger replied grimly. "Look!"

Half a mile away, riding the ridge of a dune, one . . . two . . . three . . . four . . . Four Indians, just to the north of them, and probably at the edge of the dunes.

"I can take that many standin' on my head," Harbin said. "Any time!"

"How about those?" Nora asked quietly, pointing to the south.

Five . . . no, six Indians there.

Joe Harbin looked at them. "One good drink o' water and I'll handle them too."

"Water?" Badger glanced at him. "You don't savvy Injuns, Joe. They'll let us get close, and then they'll pin us down out in the open where there's no shade, no shelter, and no chance. They'll have water. They'll drink, they'll stay out of rifle shot, and they'll wait . . . like buzzards, for us to die."

Nevertheless they moved on, wanting at any cost to get out of the sand hills.

"We could wait at the foot of the hills," Nora said, "find a place in the shade. It would be late afternoon before the sun got to us."

"And then?" Joe's tone was sarcastic.

The answer to that was obvious. If they waited, they would die. And if they tried for the shore, they would die.

"Answer to that is," Harbin muttered, replying to what Badger had said, "don't let ourselves get pinned down. We got to keep going. If they want to set on a water hole they got to fight us for it."

The pack horse went down, struggled, and failed to get up. "Cut the pack loose," Badger said, "and load the gold on the *grulla*."

When they went on, the pack horse still lay there. But Nora knew that when the coolness of night came the horse would get up, and somehow it would get to the edge of the sea, where it would find water at one of the water holes near the shore.

The sand hill broke off sharply and before them lay the coastal plain. Now they could feel the coolness of the Gulf, though it was five miles off at this point.

"We better rest," Badger muttered through broken lips. "We'd stand a better chance."

DAN RODELO DRANK deep of the cold water at the base of the Sierra Blanca. He drank, and drank again.

He removed his shirt and bathed his chest and shoulders. And all the while he was thinking hard.

By now they might have reached the Gulf, but he thought not. Perhaps Tom Badger could have, but there was no telling about Harbin. He was impulsive, dangerous, and tyrannical. Badger would play second fiddle to Harbin, waiting for his chance.

Seated in the cool shade of the rocks near the tank, Rodelo went to work on the battered canteen. Though a bullet had gone through it, he had an idea he might plug the holes well enough to keep some water in the canteen.

The weblike skeletons of the cholla that he tried to use crumbled in his fingers. Nor could he do much with a piece of ironwood that he found. He had neither time nor patience to carve that very hard wood into the necessary shape. The result was that he cut from a sahuaro cactus a plug for each hole, then filled the canteen. A little water leaked, but as the cactus plug swelled, it leaked no longer.

Carefully, he cleaned his guns, wiping each cartridge free of dust, running a rag through the barrels, checking the action then reloading.

Finding a hidden shadowed place among the rocks, he slept again. When he awakened the sun was already high and hot. His canteen was still full; he sat on a rock and studied the way he must go.

He was, he was sure, near the southern end of the area of great dunes, and might save time in the long run by scouting south, but he did not know how far he would have to go. After considerable thought he decided to strike out across the dunes, holding to as direct a line as possible.

He was so close to the Sierra that he could not pick

out any distinctive peak, but far up the side of the mountain he saw a white scar, apparently a deep cut made by run-off water. Choosing this as a means of holding his course, he took up his rifle, shouldered the canteen, and started off at a steady walk.

He continued to check the white scar on the mountain, looking back and keeping it directly behind him, but when he had gone perhaps half a mile, he chose a peak that would be even better as a guide. The first mile was the easiest, following much of the way along the high side of a dune where the sand had packed well. He made good time—not so good as a man might make on hard ground, but not much slower.

After that it was a struggle. Soft sand that slid back, losing one step out of three. But he was familiar with shifting sand, and he chose his way with care. After about an hour of walking, he believed he had made almost two miles, and now he could smell the sea plainly.

A moment later he heard the first shot. It seemed to come from the north, and at first he was not sure that it was a shot, yet what other sound could it be in this lonely, desolate land?

He heard no more shots and kept on, adding half a mile to his distance. Sliding down one dune, he climbed another at an angle, and when he reached the top he lay down on the sand. It burned his flesh, but he lay there a moment, looking ahead. Then he took a long, comfortable drink, and moved on again.

Topping out on a high pinnacle of sand that probably was the shroud for some buried granite or lava peak, he saw the sea. The blue was still far off, beautiful in the afternoon sun and the clear air. Then he spotted them, a small cluster of dark dots on the expanse of the desert.

Between the great dunes and the shore lay flat land with good patches of galleta grass and scattered mesquite or cacti. There were patches of dry lake, bare of vegetation for the most part, and, of course, the creosote bush everywhere.

At that distance he could not make out who was who, seeing them only as several dots in a cluster. Some distance away, on all sides, were the Yaquis. They were well back out of range, it seemed, and they were just waiting.

Well, Hat was in no hurry. He had them now where he had wanted them all the while. He had them out on the flat land without much shelter from bullets and no shelter from the sun.

He could afford to wait.

CHAPTER 13

AFTER SOME SEARCHING, Rodelo saw a route to the flat by which he could not be seen by the Indians. He was quite sure they were not expecting him, but he dared take no chances. He got to lower ground, took a long pull on the canteen, and then chose the shallow wash by which some of the water from Pinacate found its way to the sea.

He walked across several yards of flat ground to get to it, hoping that the Indians, a good mile or more away, would be too occupied with their quarry to see him. Once in the shallow wash, aware that he had little cover, he started off at a brisk walk. From time to time he heard a shot.

He knew what was happening. Hat was trying to draw fire from the surrounded group. He wanted to keep them worried, keep them from making a desperate try to break out of the trap. He also wanted them to expend their ammunition and their energy.

Dan Rodelo knew just how much of a gamble he was taking, and how slight were his chances, but the girl he loved was out there, and the gold that would prove him an honest man. Whatever his future might be, he knew he could not face the world without proving his innocence of crime. . . . And he wanted that girl.

But there was something else. He had never backed

away from a fight, once the issue had been faced, the battle joined. He could not back away from this one; and this was a fight he had to win.

He knew he was being a fool; he knew the odds were high that he was probably within a few hours, perhaps even a few minutes, of his death. He knew that even should he get Badger and Harbin out of the corner they were in, it would still mean shooting it out with them.

He followed along the wash, where the sand was still hard packed from the last rain. He was out of sight, but he believed he was some distance away: There had been no shot in several minutes, when he rounded a corner of the wash that was masked by mesquite and found himself face to face with an Indian.

The Yaqui wore a band around his head, and an old blood-stained army coat. He had been creeping up the bank when he heard Rodelo's step.

Rodelo was holding his Winchester in both hands ready for a quick shot, but the Yaqui was so close there was no chance to fire. He jerked the end of the barrel up hard, driving for the spot where chin and throat meet. The end of the barrel struck, and the Indian's cry was caught in a gagging, choking sound, horrible to hear. He staggered back and Rodelo followed in remorselessly, giving him a wicked smash to the head with the rifle butt driven by both hands.

The Yaqui went to the sand, and Rodelo leaned over and stripped him of his cartridge belt. He carried the second Winchester along with him.

He saw the two Indians almost at once, fifty yards off and half hidden by the sand bank. He dropped the dead Indian's rifle and brought up his own as the Yaquis caught sight of him. He saw them start to lift their rifles, but he was already firing.

His first shot, a snap shot but with enough time, was a direct hit. He saw one Indian stagger a few steps, then fall. His second shot glanced off the other Indian's rifle and went along his arm, leaving a streak behind it. The Indian dropped to one knee and fired back. Rodelo's third and fourth shots smashed him in the chest and neck.

Then Rodelo went up the wash at a run, carrying the extra rifle. His advantage was now gone, and from this moment it would be a hunting party, and he would be the game. How many Indians remained he did not know, but it was a safe guess to estimate it at ten or a dozen—far too many.

IN THE TINY hollow behind low mesquite brush where there was only partial concealment and sparse cover, Joe Harbin crouched with his gun in hand. Badger, his shoulder carrying the bloody scratch of a bullet, was nearby.

"What's goin' on out there?" Harbin muttered. "We got comp'ny."

"That will be Dan Rodelo," Nora said coolly.

Harbin looked around at her. "Like hell!" he said. "Nobody could cross that amount of country without water."

There was no further sound for several minutes, and then Harbin saw an Indian moving swiftly through the brush, his attention not on them, but directed toward some other object. He was a young warrior, and he had momentarily forgotten one enemy in concentrating on another. He was a very young warrior who would grow no older.

Joe Harbin saw him drop to the ground, and waited. The Indian had made one mistake in forgetting his first enemy, and having made one mistake he might make a second and get up from the sheltered position into which he had dropped. An older warrior would have crept along the ground and then gotten up some yards from where he had hit the ground.

The young Yaqui had been taught all that, and had done it many times in practice, but right now he forgot. Intent upon Dan Rodelo, whom he could see edging along the shallow wash, he raised up from his position slowly.

He felt the bullet hit and went to his knees. He felt it as one feels a sharp blow in the back at the waistline. He felt no pain, nothing. Puzzled, he started to get up, and could not. Slowly he wilted to the ground, looking unbelievingly at his legs, which no longer seemed a part of him. He tried to rise again, and felt a twinge of pain. He put a careful hand around to his back and it came away bloody. He reached a second time, and his questing fingers found the hole. The bullet had smashed through his spine, and it was now lodged somewhere inside him. He lay back and looked up at the sky. The buzzards were there, waiting.

Hat was puzzled. Somebody else had entered the fight, somebody he had not seen. There might be only one, but his common sense warned him there were more. There had been some shooting, but he had no idea who had shot, or why.

He gave the quail call that would withdraw the Indians, and slipped back to the place where they had left their horses. The Indians joined him. Four were missing. . . .

DAN RODELO CAME up to the little group, walking easily with his Winchester cradled over his arm. Another hung by a strap to his back, and he wore two extra cartridge belts. He had his own canteen and a water skin taken from a dead Indian.

He came to them out of the desert, and they watched him come. All had seen the Indians withdraw, but they knew it was only a temporary respite.

Rodelo looked around quickly. Only two horses were there, the *grulla,* loaded with the gold, and one other. Badger had been wounded slightly, and had bled quite a bit. He looked drawn and pale.

"We'd better get out of here while the going's good," Dan said, keeping his eyes on Harbin.

Harbin watched him, his eyes deep-sunken beneath his shaggy brows. "So you made it? I got to hand it to you, Danny. You got guts."

"I made it," Rodelo said. "And I'll make it all the way."

Harbin grinned at him, but it was not a pleasant grin. He took the bridle of the *grulla* and started off.

"Wait," Rodelo said. "You'd better have a drink."

Badger reached for the bag, grabbing it thirstily. Harbin held off, watching Badger drink. Rodelo knew what he was thinking—that he might have poisoned the water.

After a bit, Harbin drank, while Nora drank from the canteen.

They started on, but it was stumbling, bitter going.

They walked steadily, Dan Rodelo bringing up the rear. A fine white dust rose from the plain. Weird dust devils danced in the distance, and the sun was lost in a brassy sky. They plodded on, and there was no sound but the shuffling of their feet—only occasionally a mumbled curse or their hoarse panting. The ground before them was flat, their course straight except for minor deviations because of creosote or cacti. The two horses hung back, wanting to stop. There was no sign of the Indians.

The Indians knew they were going, and knew what was at the end of it—they could still afford to wait. They knew the white men had no place to go. Rodelo's unexpected appearance had spoiled their plan for the moment; they had tried too soon, and had tasted the bitterness of the white man's bullets, and now they would wait.

Overhead, also waiting, were the buzzards.

At last the sun was going down behind the mountains to the west behind the Gulf, spilling crimson and gold over the sky and turning to flame the rugged peaks of the Pinacate. The edge of the dunes became a dark, unending line behind them.

The sun had set when they reached the shore. . . . The boat was not there.

They stared out over the blue water. In their exhaustion and despair, they had no words for the emptiness that lay before them. They just stood silent in utter defeat.

The boat had been their goal, leading them on, drawing them, keeping them going. A haven they would reach, where they could rest, have a drink, eat cooked food once more.

Had the boat gone? Or had it never come?

"There's another bay," Nora said in a few minutes. "Right south of here."

"How far?"

"I don't know. Five miles—maybe ten miles even."

Ten miles! An impossible distance in their present condition.

The *grulla* tugged at his lead rope, and Harbin released his grip, almost without thinking. Trailing the rope, the mustang walked away along the flat plain where the tides came, and at a somewhat higher point he stopped and dipped his head out of sight.

"Water," Badger said flatly. "He's found the water hole."

They followed the mustang and gathered around the pool. It was small, the water was brackish, but it was wet and they could drink it.

"We could send up a smoke," Harbin suggested.

"They'd think it was Indians."

"What then?"

"We go on," Rodelo said. "We have no other choice. We go on tonight."

He looked at the packs. There it was, the gold he had come so far to get. There was the gold for which he had served a long, bitter year in prison—the gold he had told himself he would return to those to whom it belonged.

But what of these men? They had stolen it, or one of them had; and they had gone through a hard struggle to get away with it. How was he going to tell them what he meant to do?

The moment was near, and when he spoke he must be ready to shoot. Joe Harbin had counted too long on that gold, and no doubt Tom Badger had done his own figuring. Poor Gopher had been out of it from the beginning.

"We'd better dig in," Badger said. "Those Injuns will be comin' back."

"Can't you talk to 'em? They're your people."

Tom Badger looked at Harbin. "Are you crazy? I'm part Cherokee, and the Cherokee were eastern Injuns until the government took their land. We never even knew about these Yaquis. As far as that goes, the Injuns were always at war with one another—it was their favorite sport. They'd take my scalp as quick as yours."

They worked with pieces of shell and scooped out a trench, throwing up a wall of sand. It wasn't much, but it was something.

Badger glanced over at Rodelo. "You know where they'll camp?"

"North . . . that's the only place I know of with water. There's two or three springs on the shore to the north of here."

"D'you think that boat might be in the other bay?"

"If it came at all, and if it hasn't gone back, that's where it will be."

Joe Harbin drank the brackish water. He studied Dan Rodelo. "I don't figure you," he said. "You've come a long way for nothing."

Rodelo looked at him and said nothing, but he could feel the showdown coming.

"You figured we might cut you in for a piece of it, is that the idea? You want a piece of the take?"

Rodelo smiled. "I want it all, Joe. Every last bit of it."

Harbin chuckled. "Well, you're honest. I'll say that for you."

"That's just it, Joe. I'm honest."

They looked at him now. "What's that mean?" Badger said.

"I went to prison for a year simply because when they caught Joe Harbin I was riding alongside of him . . . I just happened to meet up with him on the trail. I didn't know there had been a holdup, but I had worked at the mine, I knew the gold was going up the trail. The jury figured it was too much of a coincidence."

"So you got stuck," Joe said. "Well, what of it?"

"I am going to take the gold back to them, Joe, and I'm going to rub their noses in it. I'm going to show them what a bunch of two-bit fair-weather friends they were, and then I'm going to ride away."

They stared at him, nobody speaking. Nora Paxton could hear the slow, measured beat of her heart. Suddenly Joe Harbin said, "You figured to murder us and take the gold?"

"No. I figured the Indians might do that for me, or the desert. Failing that, I thought I might come up with a plan that would get the gold without anybody being hurt."

"Now, there's a good lad," Harbin said. "He'd take our gold and not hurt us! Why, you damn fool! Who would buy a story like that?"

"I might," Badger said. "Or once upon a time I might have."

"Tell you what," Rodelo suggested. "Suppose I give you each a thousand dollars? We'll call it reward money for helping to recover it."

"Generous, ain't he?" Harbin sneered. "You ride off with our gold and leave us settin' with a thousand each! You got gall, kid, but you're in the wrong business. You ought to be a con man or a gambler."

He looked over at Nora. "Did you know about this?"

"Some of it. I believe he's telling the truth. I believe he intends to return it."

Harbin had the saddlebags behind him on the sand. He put a hand on them. "You forget it, Rodelo. You'll never lay a hand on a cent of this."

"How about some coffee?" Nora suggested. "We could take a chance on a fire. They know where we are, anyway."

Nobody paid any attention. Harbin was looking at Rodelo, and Dan could see he was ready. "How about it, kid? You going to try me? You want a piece of the action right now?"

Dan Rodelo smiled stiffly. It was an effort to smile because his lips were cracked and his face was stiff with dust, but he made it. "No, Joe, not yet. I'm going to need you for those Indians, and you're going to need me."

"We've got to get out of here," Badger said. "I think the coffee is a right idea. We'll have us a fire, make coffee, and then we'll build up the fire some an' ease out of here. We can walk in the water . . . those tide flats stretch quite a ways out. We can get on over to that other bay."

They kept well back from the fire, although it was screened by the mound of sand they had piled up. Nora made coffee, and they drank it slowly, savoring every drop. All of them needed food, but thirst had taken the edge from their appetites. What they wanted was liquid, in any form. The coffee brightened them up, and when the time came to move out they started cautiously, Tom going first and taking the horses. They reached the edge of the water together and started along, walking single file.

The Indians came out of the night suddenly. There

was a flash of a gun and a horse went down, and Dan Rodelo swung his Winchester, firing at the flash. He sprang aside, hit the ground flat-footed and fired at another flash, then dropped to the sand and rolled over behind the dead horse, firing again quickly.

He emptied his rifle and fired the Indian's gun, and when that was empty, calmly reloaded his own. Then came a lull. Somebody was beside him and suddenly the man spoke. It was Tom Badger.

"That straight about you comin' after the gold?"

"I told the truth, Tom." He paused and then added, "I never had much, Tom, but I was working into something back there. I was making a place for myself, and then I had to fall in with Joe on the trail after that holdup."

"Tough," Badger said.

They waited a moment. Then Badger asked, "D'you think we got anybody?"

"Uh-huh . . . one, maybe two."

"No tellin' in the dark, like this." After a pause he added, "I got a hunch, kid. I got a hunch I'm not goin' to make it."

"You're crazy. If anybody makes it, you will."

A few hundred yards east of them the Indians drew together. Yuma John was feeling disgusted. "I think it is finish," he said. "I want no more. Too many die."

"They are but men," Hat said.

"We are men also," Yuma John replied. "I think it is well to wait for another time."

"No," Hat said. "These I will have."

"I go," Yuma insisted. "Who goes with me?"

Two of the Indians joined him. When they had gone, Hat looked at the others. Four were still with him. Well, it was fewer with whom to divide, but it would go hard with him when he returned home. He had always been successful, and the young men had sought every chance to ride with him. Now they would say his luck was gone.

Hat led the way back toward the beach, where they found a dead horse and a few tracks. Their quarry was gone. Hat started on, leading the way.

The ambush should have succeeded. He had recognized the trick of the fire for what it was, and they had gone ahead and waited for the white men to come. They heard them walking at the water's edge but had miscalculated in the darkness. Several of his men must have shot at the horse, wasting bullets. The return fire had killed another man.

"Look," one of the young Yaquis said.

There was a darkness on the sand . . . blood. Hat lifted his head and looked after them. One of them was wounded, and had been hit hard.

Joe Harbin discovered it at almost the same instant, and a quarter of a mile further along the beach. Tom Badger was lagging, hanging to the side of the *grulla*.

"Tom? What the hell?"

"I caught one."

Harbin paused. "Bad?"

"Don't let them get me, Joe. I don't want them to cash me in."

"They won't."

"I mean it."

Dan Rodelo fell back. They had reached the point—what was it called? Sea Lion Bluff. . . .

"Let's stop here," he said. "We can see the bay. It's high here, and we can run up a signal, make a fire, or something."

"Them Injuns," Tom said, "they'll be comin' along."

"Why not lay for them?" Joe Harbin said. "We ain't likely to find a better place."

There were rocks along the shore, and on the outer edge of the bluff some sea lions had gathered, justifying the name of the point. Among the rocks and brush, with the bulk of the bluff rising behind them, they waited.

There was a rustling of surf . . . the tide was out . . . there was muttering and movement among the sea lions only a short distance away. Nora huddled close to Rodelo and whispered, scarcely moving her lips. "What will we do?"

"Wait," he said.

"Tom?" It was Harbin. "Where you hit?"

"In the belly."

Harbin swore.

Suddenly Nora spoke. "Dan, there's a light out there! On the water!"

They all saw it then. It was well out, and plain to be seen. Undoubtedly the boat lay at anchor and in swinging with the tide it had turned, showing the light.

"We made it," Tom said. "That'll be Isacher's boat."

Minutes passed. There was subdued movement from the sea lions, but nothing else. The blackness of the bluff would give perfect concealment for their small party, and any sound of movement would be laid to the sea lions.

Rodelo shifted his Winchester. He had only the one rifle, fully loaded now. The other, a poor sort of weapon, he had left back on the beach. He had examined the belts with his fingers and knew he had at least seventy rounds of ammunition, all .44's, and they could be used in either the rifle or the six-shooter he carried.

They heard the whisper on the sand before the Indians came into view, and when they did come they were only a suggestion of movement in the darkness, a shadow on the pale sand. No figure was distinct.

Nora whispered suddenly, "Joe . . . *don't!* The boat is out there. Maybe in the morning we can get aboard without a fight."

He shook her off. "Not now . . . we wouldn't have a chance."

He lifted his rifle, and Tom Badger, lying on his stomach in the cold sand, did likewise. Behind a rock Rodelo eased his own gun into position.

It might have been some movement, some glint of light on a gun barrel, but suddenly Hat hissed a sharp warning.

Instantly, Joe's rifle roared, followed by smashing reports, like echoes, from Badger and Rodelo.

A man screamed, a horse plunged, snorting, and the answering fire came quickly, stabbing flame toward the thundering rifles of the three men on the beach.

There was no question of picking targets, for there were no targets, only a confusion of movement and the flames as the Indians fired. The three men were on the ground, offering only their own gunfire for target, their bodies merged into the blackness of the bluff behind them.

Suddenly the firing ceased, there was the drum of racing hoofs. Joe shot once more, after the vanishing horse.

Then silence. . . .

Only lapping water, a faint stir of wind. Overhead bright stars that hung in the darkness above them.

"What do we do now?" Nora asked.

"We wait," Joe Harbin said grimly.

From the sand there came a low moan, then a subdued gasp. . . .

"Joe?" Tom Badger's voice was weak. "Joe, let the kid have the gold. Let him take it back. It ain't worth it."

"Sure," Harbin replied easily. "Don't worry about it. I was thinkin' the same thing."

CHAPTER 14

THE GULF LAY like a sheet of steel in the first gray light. Far out on the water lay the low black hull of a ketch, her two black bare poles pointing thin fingers at the sky.

On the sand, their bodies twisted in death, lay four Indians. Hat was not there.

Dan Rodelo stood up slowly, his muscles cramped from his position and from the dampness of the night. He picked up his rifle and wiped the moisture from the barrel.

"We'd better light a signal fire," Nora suggested. "They might leave without us."

They gathered driftwood. Only Tom lay still. "How is he?" Rodelo asked.

"Gone. You heard him—that was when he passed on."

Joe Harbin looked down at Badger. "He was a good man, and a good partner. I'd never have made it through the first year without him. He was always talkin' me down when I was ready to blow my top."

He glanced at Rodelo. "You seen me enough. You know I got a short fuse."

He lay the sticks in position, ripped a corner from his shirt for tinder, felt in his pockets. "You got a match?"

Dan reached for his shirt pocket, and Joe Harbin went for his gun. It was a difference of six inches in the position of their gun hands, and Joe Harbin was fast.

His hand dropped, gripped, the gun slid smoothly out and the muzzle came level in one perfectly timed movement, a result of long practice that had left dead men behind him.

His gun muzzle came level but something struck him hard in the side, and with a startled realization he saw Dan Rodelo was shooting.

The second shot followed the first so fast that he was turned in his tracks, his own shot drilling into the sand almost at his toes. He backed up and sat down hard on a rock, his six-shooter hanging from his fingers.

"You told Badger you'd let me have the gold," Rodelo said mildly.

"Hell, he was dyin'—it made him feel better. You didn't figure I'd fall for that, did you?"

"He was trying to save your bacon, Joe. He knew what was coming. You see, there in the past few days I think he figured out who I was."

"You?" Harbin was holding his side where the blood welled out around his hand.

"I was a kid outlaw-gunfighter back in Texas before I saw it wasn't getting me any place. That job at the mine, that was my first real job."

"That Badger," Joe Harbin said wonderingly, "always talkin' me out of it, even with his last breath. I should have listened." He was breathing now with long, shuddering gasps.

"You better light that fire," he said suddenly. Then, "Say, that boat's makin' sail?"

Rodelo turned sharply to look seaward and too late heard the click of the drawn-back hammer. He dove headfirst onto the sand, heard the roar of a gun, felt sand bite into his face. And then he was rolling over and came up shooting.

Three times he triggered the Colt, and with each shot Joe Harbin's body jerked; it rolled slowly off the rock to the sand.

White-faced and shaky, Rodelo got to his feet and looked at Nora. "That was close," he said. Wonderingly, he looked down at Harbin. "He never quit trying."

"I'll light the fire," Nora said.

She took his matches and stooped down. When she saw the flames take hold and the column of smoke lift toward the sky, she got up and walked along the side of the bluff, and dug into a crevice in the rocks. The box she brought out was rusted and old, but still solid.

"I remember the place," she said. "This is what I came for. All there is of the family I once had."

"They've lowered a boat," Rodelo said.

He picked up the sacks of gold and walked down the beach with them as the boat came in close. Two men were in the boat.

"You Isacher?" one asked.

"He's dead . . . killed some time back, trying to escape. I'm takin' his place."

"I don't know about that," the man protested. "I was to get twenty bucks a day, and—"

"You'll get that, and an extra twenty if you'll bury those two men at sea."

"Why do that? Nobody'll ever find 'em."

"There's an Indian up there who claims a fifty-buck bounty on each prisoner he takes in, dead or alive. They didn't want to go back."

"Twenty bucks? Sure enough."

He glanced at the heavy sacks Dan lifted into the boat. "What's that?"

"Trouble, friend. Too much trouble. You just forget it."

"I got to be an old man mindin' my own business. It's already forgot."

Nora got into the boat, and Dan walked to the *grulla* and slipped the bridle off. "All right, boy, you're free. You go on back to Sam, if you want, and we'll come and get you one of these days. If you don't do that, you just run wild."

He slapped the mustang on the hip and walked away, trying not to show how much he minded.

The horse looked after him, then trotted off a few steps toward Pinacate. He stopped and looked back to make sure he was right. Dan Rodelo was getting into the boat.

Taking his position in the bow of the boat, Rodelo could look shoreward, and he saw Hat come down out of the desert and ride to the shore at Sea Lion Bluff. The Indian sat his horse, looking around, then rode off slowly.

"Wherever you go," Nora was saying, "I want to go with you."

"All right," he said.

She held the rusted box tightly in her hand, but somehow it no longer seemed so important.

WHAT IS LOUIS L'AMOUR'S LOST TREASURES?

Louis L'Amour's Lost Treasures is a project created to release some of the author's more unconventional manuscripts from the family archives.

Currently included in the project are *Louis L'Amour's Lost Treasures: Volume 1*, published in the fall of 2017, and *Volume 2*, which will be published in the fall of 2019. These books contain both finished and unfinished short stories, unfinished novels, literary and motion picture treatments, notes, and outlines. They are a wide selection of the many works Louis was never able to publish during his lifetime.

In 2018 we will release *No Traveller Returns*, L'Amour's never-before-seen first novel, which was written between 1938 and 1942. In the future, there may be a selection of even more L'Amour titles.

Additionally, many notes and alternate drafts to Louis's well-known and previously published novels and short stories will now be included as "bonus feature" postscripts within the books that they relate to. For example, the Lost Treasures postscript to *Last of the Breed* will contain early notes on the story, the short story that was discovered to be a missing piece of the novel, the history of the novel's inspiration and creation, and information about unproduced motion picture and comic book versions.

An even more complete description of the Lost Treasures project, along with a number of examples of what is in the books, can be found at louislamourslosttreasures.com. The website also contains a good deal of exclusive material, such as even more pieces of unknown stories that were too short or too incomplete to include in the Lost Treasures books, plus personal photos, scans of original documents, and notes on the Sackett, Chantry, and Talon family series.

All of the works that contain Lost Treasures project materials will display the Louis L'Amour's Lost Treasures banner and logo.

LOUIS L'AMOUR'S LOST TREASURES

POSTSCRIPT

By Beau L'Amour

Kid Rodelo is one of several examples of my father's symbiotic relationship with the motion picture industry.

Part of the reason Louis chose to live in Los Angeles was the possibility of working in film. Having a secondary market for his prose work close at hand no doubt paid the bills more often than I'm aware of. Early on, he was certainly attracted to the lifestyle, but in the long run he discovered it really wasn't as good a fit as he had imagined. Writing film and TV scripts required a particular set of skills that he didn't want to take the time to acquire, and the cost of Hollywood's glamour is rather strict obedience to its culture—and Dad was never very good at obeying those sorts of rules.

To make the most of what the entertainment industry had to offer, and yet still play the game in a manner he could tolerate, Dad needed to position himself just outside the boundaries of studio or network control. That meant marketing the film and TV rights to his stories and novels as well as selling concepts or treatments, like *East of Sumatra* and *Stranger on Horseback*, without getting bogged down in the endless second-guessing of the screenwriting process.

In addition, he created novelizations of studio-conceived movies, like *How the West Was Won,* and executed projects like *Sitka,* or "The Rock Man" (*Louis L'Amour's Lost Treasures: Volume* 2), which were written at the behest of a studio or celebrity so the idea could be developed into screenplay form.

He also wrote a number of books like *Hondo* (a novelization of the film based on his short story "Gift of Cochise"), *The Shadow Riders, High Lonesome* (a novelization of the film *Four Guns to the Border,* based on his story "In Victorio's Country"), and this book, *Kid Rodelo,* a novelization of the film based on yet another L'Amour short story, "Desperate Men."

In these cases, Louis created the initial, underlying concept, often as a short story or movie treatment. That concept was produced as a film, and *then* Dad went on to write a novel which followed the release of the movie. Except for *How the West Was Won,* I believe all of these novelizations (even *Hondo*) were projects that Louis personally set up with his publishers, rather than being books which were directly commissioned by the movie studios. When it came to novelizations Dad was very much the driving force rather than just a gun for hire.

There are several different reasons for this approach, and it's completely possible that any or all of them were in effect at different times for each of these titles. The first reason was that in the days when the magazine business was collapsing, quite a few short stories, like "Desperate Men," failed to sell to his traditional contacts in publishing. Instead of trying to make inroads with editors he did not know, Dad would hand a project off to

Mauri Grashin, his movie agent. In the world of publishing, he had no equally trusted representative.

The next element was that while he might not try to sell a movie treatment to a book publisher for an advance, once a film was in the works, it would have been foolish not to take advantage of the publicity the film would generate for a novel. Throughout most of his career, every opportunity needed to be exploited to the fullest.

He may also have just wanted the last word. Dad never cared much about how his books were portrayed on the screen. He knew that film and prose were vastly different mediums and required different approaches to telling the story. He was also aware that the filmmaking process is rife with political pressures, which unfortunately tend to express themselves in changes to the script. But that lack of concern didn't mean he didn't want to have *his* version, a novel, out for the public to enjoy. Most of the time he wrote the book without ever reading a script or seeing the film. He didn't consider himself to be in competition with the movies or to be trying to correct their mistakes; he just wanted to do his own version.

The first certain reference I have found to the title "Desperate Men" is from January of 1949. An earlier journal entry shows up in February of '48 referencing a story called "Desert Mathematics," a title which suggests a theme Louis experimented with many times in his career: a group of hard characters thrown together in a life-and-death situation with a certain amount of money; the fewer survivors, the more cash would be available for the rest. It is the same scenario that is present in "Desperate Men."

However, "Desert Mathematics" was finished and submitted for publication in '48. Perhaps it was rejected and Louis began rewriting it the next year as "Desperate Men." Or perhaps it was a different story altogether. As a famous fictional detective once said: "If you can't stand not knowing, you're in the wrong business."

Whether "Desert Mathematics" was or was not an early title, by the end of 1950 Dad had finished "Desperate Men." For a guy who could write a novel in a month or two, this was a very long time for him to spend on one project. On a number of occasions he remarked that he had written "a couple of desultory pages" before putting it aside, or that it was not going well. But one of the aspects of Dad's creative process that has become clear to me during my work on the Lost Treasures project is that many of these stories took a good deal longer than I thought. Generally, Louis threw himself into a situation hoping that inspiration would strike. When it did he could work very quickly, and when it didn't he worked on other things but kept himself involved by returning to the project occasionally, biding his time, waiting for the moment to be right.

In early 1951 "Desperate Men" was rejected by *Esquire, Argosy, Adventure,* and *Better Publications.* This was, financially, probably the toughest year in the latter half of my father's life. The magazine business was in turmoil, and competition among the surviving publications was fierce. Dad only had so much time, and most of it needed to be spent writing rather than trying to find new prospective markets, so he put this story in a box and moved on. "Desperate Men" was finally released in the collection *End of the Drive* in 1997. Below is the full text of "Desperate Men," as well as the story of how fifteen years later it was turned into both a feature film and a novel, as *Kid Rodelo*.

DESPERATE MEN

They were four desperate men, made hard by life, cruel by nature, and driven to desperation by imprisonment. Yet the walls of Yuma Prison were strong and the rifle skill of the guards unquestioned, so the prison held many desperate men besides these four. And when prison walls and rifles failed, there was the desert, and the desert never failed.

Fate, however, delivered these four a chance to test the desert. In the early dawn the land had rolled and tumbled like an ocean storm. The rocky promontory over the river had shifted and cracked in an earthquake that drove fear into the hearts of the toughest and most wicked men in Arizona. For a minute or two the ground had groaned and roared, dust rained down from cracks in the roofs of the cells, and in one place the perimeter wall had broken and slid off, down the hillside. It was as if God or the Devil had shown them a way.

Two nights later, Otteson leaned his shaven head closer to the bars. "If you're yellow, say so! I say we can make it! If Isager says we can make it through the desert, I say we go!"

"We'll need money for the boatmen." Rodelo's voice was low. "Without money we will die down there on the shores of the gulf."

All were silent, three awaiting a word from the fourth. Rydberg knew where the Army payroll was buried. The government did not know, the guards did not know, only Rydberg. And Otteson, Isager, and Rodelo knew he knew.

He was a thin, scrawny man with a buzzard's neck and a buzzard's beak for a nose. His bright, predatory eyes indicated his hesitation now. "How . . . how much would it take?" he asked.

"A hundred," Otteson suggested, "not more than two. If we had that much we could be free."

Free . . . no walls, no guards, no stinking food. No sweating one's life out with backbreaking labor under the blazing sun. Free . . . women, whiskey, money to spend . . . the click of poker chips, the whir of the wheel, a gun's weight on the hip again. No beatings, no solitary, no lukewarm, brackish drinking water. Free to come and go . . . a horse between the knees . . . women . . .

He said it finally, words they had waited to hear. "There's the Army payroll. We could get that."

The taut minds of Otteson, Rodelo, and Isager relaxed slowly, easing the tension, and within the mind of each was a thought unshared.

Gold . . . fifteen thousand in gold coins for the taking! A little money split four ways, but a lot of money for one!

Otteson leaned his bullet head nearer. "Tomorrow night"--his thick lips barely moved as he whispered--"tomorrow night we'll go out. If we wait longer they'll have the wall repaired."

"There's been guards posted ever since the quake," Rodelo protested.

Otteson laughed. "We'll take care of them!" From under the straw mattress he drew a crude, prison-made knife. "Rydberg can take care of the other with his belt."

Cunningly fashioned of braided leather thongs, it concealed a length of piano wire. When the belt was removed and held in the hands it could be bent so the loop of the steel wire projected itself, a loop large enough to encircle a man's head . . . then it could be jerked tight and the man would die.

Rodelo leaned closer. "How far to the gold?"

"Twenty miles east. We'll need horses."

"Good!" Otteson smashed a fist into a palm. "East is good! They'll expect us to go west into California. East after the gold, then south into the desert. They'd never dream we'd try that! It's hot as sin and dry as Hades, but I know where the water holes are!"

Their heads together, glistening with sweat in the hot, sticky confines of their cells, they plotted every move, and within the mind of three of the men was another plot: to kill the others and have the gold for himself.

"We'll need guns." Rydberg expressed their greatest worry. "They'll send Indians after us."

The Indians were paid fifty dollars for each convict returned alive--but they had been paid for dead convicts, too. The Yaquis knew the water holes, and fifty dollars was twice what most of them could make in a month if they could find work at all.

"We'll have the guns of the two guards. When we get to Rocky Bay, we'll hire a fisherman to carry us south to Guaymas."

The following day their work seemed easy. The sun was broiling and the guards unusually brutal. Rydberg was knocked down by a hulking giant named Johnson. Rydberg just brushed himself off and smiled. It worried Johnson more than a threat. "What's got into him?" he demanded of the other guards. "Has he gone crazy?"

Perryman shrugged. "Why worry about it? He's poison mean, an' those others are a bad lot, too. Otteson's worst of all."

"He's the one I aim to get," Johnson said grimly, "but did you ever watch the way he lifts those rocks? Rocks two of us couldn't budge he lifts like they were so many sacks of spuds!"

It was sullen dark that night; no stars. There was thunder in the north and they could hear the river. The heat lingered and the guards were restless from the impending storm. At the gap where the quake had wrecked the wall were Perryman and Johnson. They would be relieved in two hours by other guards.

They had been an hour on the job and only now had seated themselves. Perryman lit a cigarette and leaned back. As he straightened to say something to Johnson he was startled to see kicking feet and clawing hands, but before he could rise, a powerful arm came over his shoulder, closing off his breath. Then four men armed with rifles and pistols went down the side of Prison Hill and walked eastward toward the town.

One hour before discovery. That was the most they could expect, yet in half that time they had stolen horses and headed east. Otteson had been shrewd. He had grabbed Perryman's hat from the ground. Both Isager and Rodelo had hats of a sort. Rydberg was without any covering for his shaven head.

Two hours after their escape they reached the adobe. Rydberg led the way inside the ruin, and they dug up the gold from a far corner. Each man took a sack, and then they turned their horses to the south and the desert.

"Each year," Otteson said, "the

fishermen come to Rocky Bay. They live there while they fish, and then return to their homes down the gulf. Pablo told me, and he said to keep Pinacate on my left and head for the coast at Flat Hill. The bay is on a direct line between the hill and the coast."

Pablo had been killed by a blow on the head from a guard's gun, but he had been planning escape with Otteson. Dawn came at last and the clouds slid away leaving the sun behind . . . and the sun was hot.

From the Gila River to the Mexican border there was nothing. Only desert, cacti, rocks, and the sun, always the sun. There was not even water until one almost reached the border. Water was found only in *tinajas,* basins that captured rain and retained it until [it was] finally evaporated by the sun. Some of the *tinajas* were shaded and held the water for a long time, and in others there was just sand. Sometimes water impregnated the sand at the bottom. These things a man must know to survive on that Devil's trail.

Their route from the Gila to the border was approximately fifty miles as the buzzard flies, but a man does not ride as the buzzard flies, not even in a lonely and empty land. There are clusters of rock, broken lava, upthrust ledges, and clumps of cacti. And there are always, inevitably, arroyos. Seventy miles would be closer to the truth, seventy miles of desert in midsummer.

The border was a vague line which in theory left them free of pursuit, but in 1878 officers of the law often ignored lines of demarcation--and the Indians did not notice them at all. Actually, the border was their halfway point, for they had a rough distance of one hundred and forty miles to traverse.

Behind them two guards lay dead, and the hostler only lived because Rodelo was not, by nature, a killer. Rodelo had the sleeping man's hands and feet tied before he got his eyes open. Then he gagged and left him. They stole four horses and three canteens and filled the canteens at the pump. Otteson, Rydberg, and Isager took it for granted the hostler had been killed.

They rode hard for twenty miles, and then they had the added weight of the gold. Otteson knew the way from Pablo and he pointed it out occasionally as they rode. But he did not offer his back to his companions.

Four battered and desperate men headed south under the glaring sun. Dust lifted, they sweated, and their lips grew dry. They pushed their horses, for distance was important. Otteson called a halt, finally. He was a heavy man and the hard riding sapped the strength of his horse.

"Where is it we're gonna find water?" Isager noted the hesitation before Otteson replied. Isager knew the desert, but not this area. Otteson only had the knowledge Pablo had given him and he didn't want to tell too much.

"Near Coyote Peak there's water. Maybe ten miles yet."

Isager tested the weight of his canteen. Rodelo drank several good gulps and returned his canteen to its place behind his saddle. Rydberg, who had brought the guard's water bottle, drank also. Otteson made a motion of drinking, but Isager watched his Adam's apple. It did not move.

Isager was a lean man, not tall, and narrow of jaw and cheekbone. He weighed one hundred and fifty pounds and carried no ounce of fat. He had been sent to Yuma after killing a marshal, which would have been his sixth notch if he had been a man for carving notches. It was noteworthy that in selecting a weapon he had taken a pistol. Isager was nothing if not practical. The pistol was his favorite weapon, and the four would be close together. By the time they had spread out to where a rifle might be useful, he would have a rifle. Of that he was positive.

Rodelo knew nothing of the desert but much of men. When younger he had sailed to the West Coast of Africa and had seen men die of the sun. He had replaced the bandanna that covered his head when working in the prison yard with a hat stolen from the livery, knowing the sun would be vicious on their shaven skulls. They depended upon Otteson, and he was not to be trusted. Isager alone he respected: he liked none of them. Rydberg did not guess what the others knew--that they would soon be minus a man.

They walked their horses now. Behind them was no dust, but pursuit was certain. It was the Indians who worried them, for fifty dollars was a lot of money to an Indian. Two hundred dollars for them all.

The air wavered and changed before

them, seeming to flow and billow with heat waves. On their right was the Gila Range, and the desert grew more rugged. Otteson watched when Rydberg drank, when he passed his hand over his bare skull, saw him put water on his head. Otteson was complacent, confident.

Isager's mouth was dry, but he did not touch the canteen. A mere swallow at dusk could do more good than a bucket now. He watched the others with cat eyes. Rydberg took another pull. The heat baked the desert and reflected in their faces like heat from a hot stove. Twice they stopped for rest, and each time it was Otteson and Isager who stopped in what little shade there was. Rydberg swayed as he dismounted.

"Hot!" he gasped. "How much farther to water?"

"Not far." Otteson looked at Rydberg's horse. It was the best.

Isager took water from his canteen and wiped out his horse's mouth and nostrils. Rodelo thought this was a good idea and did likewise.

"Let's wait until dark," Rydberg suggested. "I'm hot. My head aches. That sun is killing me."

"You want to get caught by them Injuns? Or them laws from Yuma?"

They moved on, and Rydberg's skull was pocked with sun blisters. The dust grew thicker, the air was dead, the desert a pink and red reflector for the sun. Rydberg swayed drunkenly, and Rodelo swore mentally and reflected that it must be 120 degrees or more.

Rydberg began to mutter. He pulled at his dry canteen. He tried again, shook it, and there was no sound. Otteson looked straight before him. Isager said nothing, and only Rodelo looked around as the man swayed drunkenly in his saddle.

"I'm out of water," Rydberg said. "How about a drink?"

"On the desert," Otteson said, "each man drinks his own water. You'll have to wait."

The dust and sun and thirst turned their world into a red hell of heat waves and blurred blue mountains. The hooves of their horses dragged. Rydberg muttered, and once he croaked a snatch of song. He mumbled through thin, cracked lips, and the weird face above the scraggly neck became even more buzzardlike. His skull was fiery red now, and it bobbed strangely as he weakened. Suddenly he shouted hoarsely and pointed off across the desert.

"Water!" he gabbled. "Water, over there!"

"Mirage," Rodelo said, and the others were silent, riding.

"Gimme a drink." Rydberg rode at Otteson and grabbed at his canteen.

The big man moved his horse away, striking at the skinny hand. "Go to hell," he said coldly.

Rydberg grabbed at him, lost balance, and fell heavily into the sand. He struggled to get up, then fell again.

Rodelo looked at him. His own canteen was empty. "The damn fool," Isager said, "why didn't he get him a hat?"

Nobody else spoke. Then Otteson reached for the canteen on Rydberg's horse, but Isager was closer and unhurriedly appropriated it. He also took the rifle. "Take the horse if you like," he said, "you're a heavy man."

Otteson glared at Isager, and Rodelo moved in and took the gold. "Are you going to leave him here like that?" he demanded.

Otteson shrugged. "He asked for it."

"He wouldn't live until night," Isager said. "Stay if you want."

Rodelo drew Rydberg into the shade

of an ironwood tree. Then he mounted and followed. Why had they grabbed the empty canteen and the rifle when they could have gotten their hands on Rydberg's share of the gold?

A thin shadow of doubt touched him. Then the answer was plain and he cursed himself for a fool. Nearly two hundred gold coins he now carried, and it was considerable weight. They preferred that he carry the extra gold until . . . His jaw set hard, but within him there was a cold shock of fear.

They thought he was going to die! They thought--He'd show them. From deep within him came a hard burning defiance. He'd show them.

It had been midafternoon when they left Rydberg. It was two hours later when they came up to Coyote Peak. Otteson was studying the rocks around and suddenly he turned sharply left and rode into an arroyo. Twenty minutes later they stood beside the *tinaja*.

Despair mounted within Rodelo. It was only a hollow of rock with a few gallons of water in the bottom. They filled their canteens, then watered the horses. When the horses had finished the water was gone.

"We'll rest a few hours," Isager suggested, "then go on after dark."

Isager ignored the shade and lay down on his side with his face toward the two men and his weapons and water close behind him.

Rodelo found a spot in soft sand, well back in the shadow of the rocks. He stared at the others and thought exhaustion had made them stupid. Both had relaxed upon hard, rocky ground. The least move would awaken them. They would get no rest that way. While this was soft sand. . . . He relaxed luxuriously.

He awakened with a start. It was cold, dark, and silent. With sudden panic, he sprang to his feet. "Isager!" he shouted. "Ott!" And the desert gave back only echoes. He felt for his canteen, and it was gone. He ran to where his horse had been picketed, and it, too, was gone.

He had slept and they had left him. They had taken the gold, the horse, the canteen . . . only his pistol remained.

He had that only because they had feared to awaken him.

He rushed to a rise of ground, scrambled, slipped on the rocks, and skinned his knees. Then he got to the top and stared off to the southeast. All he could see was the soft, velvety darkness, the cool of the desert night, and the unspeaking stars.

He was alone.

For the first time he was frightened. He was horribly, unspeakably frightened. Rodelo hated being alone, he feared loneliness, and he knew the power of the desert to kill.

Then his fear left him, his thoughts smoothed out, and the panic ended. They could not move fast without knowing the country better than they did. They would travel at a walk, and if they did, he might overtake them. He was younger than either, and he was strong. He had never found a trial that could test his endurance.

A glance at the stars told him they could have no more than an hour's start. How much would that mean at night in unfamiliar desert? Three miles? Five miles?

Doubt came. Could he make up the distance? They would never suspect pursuit. Suppose the day came and he was still without water? But what would waiting gain? This was not a spring, and the *tinaja* was empty.

He could wait for death, or for capture on the verge of death, or he could fight. He returned to the *tinaja* and found perhaps a cup of water in the bottom. He thrust his head into the basin and sucked it up. Then he straightened, glanced at the stars for direction, and struck out for the southeast, walking steadily.

Otteson and Isager rode side by side. Each man led a horse, and on those horses were the gold sacks. The issue between them was clear now. Isager knew he was faster with a gun, and Otteson knew it also. Therefore, the big man would wait for a moment when the killing was a sure thing.

Neither man mentioned Rydberg nor Rodelo. It was like Otteson to ignore what was past. Isager thought of Rodelo with regret--he had liked the younger man, but this was a matter of survival. They walked their horses, careful not to tire them. Once, encountering a nest of boulders, they circled some distance to get past them. Over the next two hours this allowed Rodelo to gain considerable ground.

The first day netted them sixty

miles of distance but twenty of it had been up the Gila for the gold, and the next forty angling toward the border. Daylight found them near the border and Otteson looked back. Nothing but heat waves. "They'll be coming," Isager said. "They'll find Rydberg by the buzzards. Then they'll find Rodelo. That gives them a line on us even if they don't find our trail."

Ahead of them on their right was a cluster of mesas, on their left ahead high and blue on the horizon, the bulk of Pinacate, a fifteen-mile-long ridge that towered nearly five thousand feet into the brassy sky.

The coolness left the desert as the sun lifted. Both men knew the folly of haste. Moreover they had each other to watch. Neither wanted to go ahead, and this slowed their pace.

Isager wished it had been Otteson back there rather than Rodelo. He had seen the big man get to his feet and had done likewise. Both had chosen stony ground, as a sound sleep might be their last sleep. Otteson had saddled up, glanced at the sleeping man, and then with a shrug had gathered up Rodelo's gear and horse. To stop him would mean a shoot-out, and neither knew which side Rodelo would join if awakened by gunfire. He had mounted up and taken Rydberg's horse. Neither had planned on abandoning the young man when they stopped, but this was a case of survival of the fittest and Rodelo had given them an opportunity to decrease their number by one more.

"You sure the fishermen come there at this time of the year?"

"Pablo said so. He planned to go this way himself. Rocky Bay, they call it. From Flat Hill we go right down to the water. How could a man mistake a bay? And if the fishermen aren't there, we'll wait."

Not long after that they came up to Tinajas Altas where they watered the horses and refilled their canteens. Isager looked over the back trail from beside the tanks. He saw no dust, no movement. Once he believed he saw something stir down there, but it could have been nothing more than a coyote or a mountain sheep. A horse would make dust.

They rested, drank water again, and ate a little of the hardtack and jerky they had smuggled from the prison, food hoarded against this effort. An hour passed, then a second hour. The rest meant much to them and to their horses. Otteson got up carefully, facing Isager. "Reckon we'd better move on. I won't feel safe until we're on that fishin' boat headed south."

Up on the mesa's side among the talus, something moved. Isager's quick eye saw it and recognized it in the same instant with a start of inward surprise. Otteson's back was to the talus, but he saw a flicker of something in Isager's eyes. "What's the matter?" he exclaimed, starting to turn.

He caught himself, his eyes turning ugly. "Figured I'd turn an' you'd shoot me? Don't try nothin' like that."

Rodelo was on the slope behind and slightly above Otteson and about thirty yards back from him. His face was ghastly and red, his prison jeans were torn from cacti and rocks, but he clutched a businesslike .44 in his fist. He lifted it and took careful sight, shifting his feet as he did so. A rock rolled under his foot.

Otteson whipped around, quick as a cat. His rifle blasted from the hip and he missed. He never fired again. He went down, clawing at the rocks and gravel on which he had fallen, blood staining their pink to deep crimson. Isager held his smoking Colt and looked up the slope at Rodelo.

The younger man had recovered his balance and they stared at each other over their guns.

"You might miss," Isager said. "I never do."

"Why don't you shoot, then?"

"I want company. Two can make it easier than one. Much easier than three."

"Then why didn't you let him kill me?"

"Because he wanted to kill me himself. You need me. I know the desert and you don't."

Rodelo came over the rocks, stepping carefully. "All right," he said. "Gimme water."

Isager holstered his gun. "There's the *tinaja.* Drink an' we'll push on." He looked at Rodelo with curious respect. "How'd you catch up so fast?"

"You rode around things. I walked straight to your dust. You rested. I couldn't afford to."

"Good man." Isager mounted up. Nothing was said about what happened. "If we play it smart now, we'll leave each other alone. Together we can make it through."

One thing they had not forgotten. The knowledge of the *tinajas* lay dead in the skull of Otteson.

"We'll have to make our water last. It won't be far now. That's Pinacate."

The mountain bulked before them now, and by the time the stars were out it loomed huge on the horizon. They slept that night and when they awakened, Rodelo looked around at Isager. His cheekbones were slashes of red from the sun, his eyes deep sunken. Stubble of beard covered his cheeks and his shirt was stiff with sweat and dust. "I smell the sea," he said, low-voiced. "I can smell the sea."

When they started on once more, they kept the mountain between them and the sun, saving themselves from the heat. Once they found a water hole but the mud was cracked and dry in the bottom. Isager's brown face was shadowed with red, Otteson's hat pulled low over his cold eyes.

The horses were gaunt and beaten. Several times the men dismounted and led the horses to spare them. Their hunger was a gnawing, living thing within them, and their spare canteens were dry, their own very low. The eyes of the men were never still, searching for water. Yet it was not enough to look. One had to know. In the desert water may be within a few feet and give no indication of its presence. And then, from the top of a rise, they saw the gulf!

"There it is." Rodelo stared, hollow-eyed. "Now for that bay."

A squarish flat hill was before them. They circled and saw the gulf due west of it. "S'pose that's it?" Isager asked doubtfully.

"You can see for yourself that it's a big bay." The tension between them was back: they were watching each other out of the corners of their eyes again.

Isager stood in his stirrups and looked south. Land stretched away until it ended in a point. There was a hint of sea in that direction but he was not sure. "All right," he said, "but I don't see any boats."

The plain sloping down to the bay was white with soda and salt. Long sand spits extended into the milky blue water. Here and there patches showed above the surface. "Looks mighty shallow," Rodelo said doubtfully. "Don't seem likely a boat would come in here."

Isager hefted his canteen, feeling its lightness with fear. "We'd better hunt for water."

South of them, the rocky bluff shouldered against the sky, dark and rugged. North the beach lay flat and empty . . . frightening in its emptiness. The horses stood, heads down and unmoving. The rocky bluff looked promising, but the salt on his lips frightened Isager. Behind them they heard a deep, gasping sigh and they turned. The paint packhorse was down.

It had sunk to the sand and now it lay stretched out, the hide on its flanks hanging like loose cloth in the hollows of its ribs.

Isager removed the gold from the horse, and with the gold off, it struggled to rise. Isager glanced at Rodelo, hesitant to use both hands to help the horse. "Go ahead," Rodelo said, "help him."

Together they got the horse up, and then they turned south. The salty crust crunched and broke beneath their feet. Sometimes they sank to their ankles; the horses broke through at every step. They often stopped to rest and Isager glanced at Rodelo. "We better have a truce," he said, his eyes shifting away, then back. "You couldn't make it without me."

Rodelo's lips thinned over his white teeth. "Don't need you. You knew the desert. I know the sea."

"The desert's still with us," Isager said. Suddenly the water in Rodelo's canteen was more precious than gold. He was waiting for a chance to go for his gun.

The white glare around them forced their eyes to thin slits, while soda dust settled over them in a thin cloak. They stared at each other, as wild and thin as the gaunt, skeletonlike horses, white and shadowy things that seemed to waver with unreality in the heat. The milky water, undrinkable, and taunting them, whispered secret obscenities along the blue-white beach. "There'll be a fishing boat," Isager said. "No reason to kill each other. Maybe there's water beyond that bluff."

"There'll be no boat." Rodelo stated it flatly. "This is the wrong bay."

Isager stared, blinking slowly. "Wrong bay?" he said stupidly.

"Look!" Rodelo shouted harshly.

"It's too shallow! We've come to the wrong place!"

Isager's dry tongue fought for his lips. There was no hope then.

"Give me your gun," Rodelo said, "and I'll take you there."

"So you can kill me?" Isager drew back, his eyes cold and calculating.

"I know where the bay is," Rodelo said. "Give me your gun."

Isager stared. Was it a trick? How could he actually know?

Suddenly, Rodelo shrugged. "Come on, then! I'll take my chances on you!" He pointed toward the dark bluff. "Look! That's a water sky. There's water beyond that point. Another bay!"

He took a step and a bullet kicked dust at his feet. He grabbed for his gun and whirled on Isager, but the gunfighter had already faced the hillside. Four Indians were coming down the hill, riding hard. As Rodelo turned, Isager stepped his feet apart and fired. An Indian's horse stumbled and went down, throwing the rider head over heels.

Rodelo dropped to one knee and shot under the belly of his horse. He saw an Indian drop and he fired again and missed. A bullet hit Isager and turned him half around.

He staggered, and the half-dead horse lunged clumsily away. A hoof went through the crust and the horse fell heavily and lay panting, one white sliver of bone showing through the hide of the broken leg.

Isager fell, pulled off balance by the fall of the horse, and Rodelo fired again and again. His gun muzzle wavered and the shots kicked up dust. Isager rolled over behind the downed horse. He knew from harsh experience that accuracy was more essential than speed. He steadied his gun barrel. The Indian who had been thrown was rushing him. The brown body loomed large and he could see sweat streaks on the man's chest. He squeezed off his shot and saw the Indian stumble in midstride and then pitch over on his face.

Isager pushed himself to his knees, then got up. The beach weaved slowly, sickeningly beneath him. He turned his head stiffly and looked toward Rodelo. The fallen man looked like a bundle of old clothes, but as Isager looked, the bundle moved. Rodelo uncoiled himself and got up. Blood covered his face from a cut on his cheek. He stared at his empty gun, then clumsily began feeding shells into the chambers.

Across the wavering sand the two men stared at each other, then Rodelo laughed hoarsely. "You look like hell!" he said, grinning from his heat-blasted face.

Isager's brain seemed to spin queerly and he blinked. What was the matter with him? A pain bit suddenly at his side, and he clasped the pain with his hand. His fingers felt damp and he drew them away, staring stupidly at the blood dripping from his fingers.

"You copped one," Rodelo said. "You're hit."

Isager swayed. Suddenly he knew this was it, right here on this dead-white beach washed by an ugly weedy sea. It was no way for a cowhand to cash in his chips. "Beat it," he said hoarsely. "There's more coming."

"How do you know that?"

"That's why they rushed. To get us an' claim the reward. If they'd been alone they would have taken their time." His knees felt buttery and queer. "There's one good horse. Take the gold an' beat it. I'm done in, so I'll hold them off."

He went to his knees. "Only . . ." His voice trailed off and he waited, his eyes begging Rodelo to wait a minute longer, then he managed the words, ". . . get some of that money to Tom Hopkins's wife. He . . . he was that marshal. Funny thing, funny . . . Never meant to kill him. He came at me an' it was just reflex . . . jus' . . . just drew an' shot."

"All right," Rodelo said, and he meant it. He turned and disappeared into the blinding light.

Isager lay down behind the fallen horse. He slid the rifle from its scabbard and waited.

Sheriff Bill Garden and two Apache trackers found Isager a few hours later. Gunfire from the advance party of six Yaquis had led them to this desolate beach. The convict was curled up behind a dying horse, surrounded by bright brass shells ejected from his rifle. Two of the Apache horses were gone and only one of the horses ridden by the convicts was alive. He was standing head down on the hillside not far away.

Horse tracks trailed away from the body of Isager, a faint trail toward the bluff to the south. Bill Garden glanced after them. The remaining scouts were still after the last man. He turned and looked down at Isager. "Lord a-mighty," he said. "What a place to die!"

Far off across the water there was a flash of white, a jib shaken out to catch the wind . . . a boat had left the fishing beds at Rocky Bay and was beating its way southward toward Guaymas.

An important element in the transitional era of my father's career, the time in which working in Hollywood eased his shift from writing short stories to writing novels, was his professional relationship with screenwriter Jack Natteford. Natteford was a Hollywood veteran with a career that dated back to silent movies in the teens and twenties. As far as I know Louis and Jack were not close personally, but they shared the same agent, Mauri Grashin, and they cooperated on three projects: *East of Sumatra*, *Kilkenny* (released under the horrific title *Black Jack Ketchum, Desperado*), and *Kid Rodelo*.

East of Sumatra was their first effort, but with the production of *Hondo* and Louis's finally settling into a career writing paperback originals, it was a couple of years before they followed up with anything else. Probably at the behest of Mauri, Dad dug out his copy of "Desperate Men," then created some sort of outline suggesting a few improvements for the screen and handed the project over to Jack so that he could write the script.

I think it's important to note, especially given the sort of celebrity culture that surrounds us today, that these guys were just working stiffs. My father's life was far from glamorous. He and Jack were both selling what they could to television, which was considered a very secondary market in those days, and striving to occasionally place a project in the lower echelons of the feature-film world. Dad was building a solid career writing fiction, but he would never again have a movie made that was as high-profile as *Hondo*.

Natteford's work on "Desperate Men" started in 1954, and in September of 1955 they had accepted an option from the William B. White Agency. The deal the agent was putting together likely sounded promising, because Louis and Jack optioned the story/screenplay package for a token fee. But it did not pan out, and after a six-month extension, for which a reasonable amount of money was paid, the option lapsed.

Late in 1957, the project was optioned again, this time by producers George Sherman (well known as a director of early John Wayne and Gene Autry pictures) and Jack Lamont. This deal seems to have been some kind of foreign production, because a dispute erupted over a new writer Natteford suspected had been hired in order to access foreign capital. This new screenwriter was a mysterious character named Manning O'Brine, an Irishman known for his screenplays and spy novels, who may have been a secret agent of one sort or another before, during, and after World War Two. Though this minor dustup regarding credit eventually blew over, the rights seem to have lapsed, and again the project was shelved.

Five years later, in 1963, Sherman reignited some interest in doing the story as a foreign coproduction. Although Sherman personally ended up working on another project, *Kid Rodelo* was eventually filmed by his company in Almería, Spain, in 1965, very closely crossing paths with Sergio Leone's *For a Few Dollars More.*

As soon as the film finally became a reality, my father settled in to take advantage of its release by writing the story into novel form. Although this was, in effect, a "novelization" of the movie, as mentioned above it was not the typical deal where a movie studio commissioned the book. It was Louis who arranged for it to be published as a tie-in.

For better or for worse, he chose to depart from the more grimly realistic tone of the short story, and to include elements like the character played by Janet Leigh in the movie; some of these changes may have even been included in the notes he provided to Jack Natteford when they first started the project. Although Dad hated the title *Kid Rodelo,* and had no idea what the finished project would look like other than being generally aware of Natteford's early screenplay drafts, sticking with many of the details of the movie was his idea, carefully calculated to gain him whatever publicity was available from the film.

This was still five years before Bantam started to promote Louis's work, and only ten or twelve years after the period he'd been afraid he'd soon be living on the street. Dad knew the value of publicity and was used to rustling it up himself. He had promoted boxers, both black and white, on the mean streets of Oklahoma City in the 1930s and had managed his own career as a writer. He was well aware that the push Warner Brothers had put behind *Hondo* had helped him considerably, and that his publishers were always thrilled to take advantage of a movie company's marketing campaign if they could.

In this case, the effect was negligible. The film didn't bomb, but it was hardly anything to brag about. By that time, however, Dad had other books being prepared for publication and several more in the works—he was nothing but pragmatic about the situation.

Beau L'Amour
July 2018

ABOUT LOUIS L'AMOUR

"I think of myself in the oral tradition—
as a troubadour, a village taleteller, the man in the shadows of the campfire. That's the way I'd like to be remembered—as a storyteller. A good storyteller."

It is doubtful that any author could be as at home in the world re-created in his novels as Louis Dearborn L'Amour. Not only could he physically fill the boots of the rugged characters he wrote about, but he literally "walked the land my characters walk." His personal experiences as well as his lifelong devotion to historical research combined to give Mr. L'Amour the unique knowledge and understanding of people, events, and the challenge of the American frontier that became the hallmarks of his popularity.

As a boy growing up in Jamestown, North Dakota, he absorbed all he could about his family's frontier heritage, including the story of his great-grandfather who was scalped by Sioux warriors.

Spurred by an eager curiosity and desire to broaden his horizons, Mr. L'Amour left home at the age of fifteen and enjoyed a wide variety of jobs, including seaman, lumberjack, elephant handler, skinner of dead cattle, miner, and an officer in the transportation corps during World War II. He was a voracious reader and collector of books. His personal library contained 17,000 volumes.

Mr. L'Amour "wanted to write almost from the time I could talk." After developing a widespread following for his many frontier and adventure stories written for fiction magazines, Mr. L'Amour published his first full-length novel, *Hondo,* in the United States in 1953. Every one of his more than 120 books is in print; there are more than 300 million copies of his books in print worldwide, making him one of the bestselling authors in modern literary history. His books have been translated into twenty languages, and more than forty-five of his novels and stories have been made into feature films and television movies.

His hardcover bestsellers include *The Lonesome Gods, The Walking Drum* (his twelfth-century historical novel), *Jubal Sackett, Last of the Breed,* and *The Haunted Mesa.* His memoir, *Education of a Wandering Man,* was a leading bestseller in 1989. Audio dramatizations and adaptations of many L'Amour stories are available on cassette tapes from Random House Audio.

The recipient of many great honors and awards, in 1983 Mr. L'Amour became the first novelist ever to be awarded the Congressional Gold Medal by the United States Congress in honor of his life's work. In 1984 he was also awarded the Medal of Freedom by President Reagan.

Louis L'Amour died on June 10, 1988.